NIGHTSOIL

Levi S. Peterson

NIGHT SOIL

NEW STORIES BY LEVI S. PETERSON

Signature Books   Salt Lake City   1990

"Night Soil" first appeared in *Utah Holiday* 15 (December 1985): 6-83, 88.

"Sunswath" first appeared in *Sunstone* 10 (12): 13-22.

"The Third Nephite" first appeared in *Dialogue: A Journal of Mormon Thought* 19 (Winter 1986): 159-71.

"The Newsboy" first appeared in *Weber Studies* 5 (Fall 1988): 41-57.

Dust jacket design: Brian Bean

Dust jacket illustration: Mark Robison

94 93 92 91   6 5 4 3 2

LIBRARY OF CONGRESS CATALOGING-IN-PUBLICATION DATA

Peterson, Levi S., 1933–
  Night soil: new stories / Levi S. Peterson.
    p. cm.
  ISBN 1-56085-003-5
  I. Title.
PS3566.E7694N54 1990
813'.54 — dc20   90–38313
                                                  CIP

To my brothers and sisters —

Arley, Leora, Andelin, Earland, Elwood, Lenora,
Wanda, Mary, Alma, Charles, Roald, and Leon

Contents

THE NEWSBOY

ALBERT WAS THE TOWN NEWSBOY — A SMALL, SWEET-faced, knobby-jointed kid of eleven. One August day he came out of the house wearing a baseball cap and a *Deseret News* T-shirt. He bridled an old mare and shoved a saddle onto her back. As he cinched up, the mare tried to bite him and he gave her a punch in the nose. He threw his paperbag over the cantle, stood on an upside-down grain bucket, and climbed aboard. He pulled his belt from the loops of his pants and slapped the mare on the flank. She groaned and ambled into the street.

Down the road roared an open Model A spewing gravel and stirring dust. In it were Ralph Drayton and his rowdy friends, none old enough to have a driver's license. As they careened by, one of them shouted an obscenity at Albert. He shook a fist and they laughed and shouted more dirty words.

Albert tied the mare at the back of the grocery store on Main Street and carried the paperbag around front. A bus from Salt Lake had dropped off a big bundle of the *Deseret News* and a small bundle of the *Salt Lake Tribune*. Only backsliders and gentiles subscribed to the *Tribune*. Albert knelt, clipped the wires, and counted both bundles. Exactly the expected number. The headlines said the Japanese had surrendered.

Cull Stevens, owner of the store, came out carrying a scoop shovel. The boy said, "Look here. The war's over."

"Everybody knows that," Cull said. "It's been on the radio all day."

"Nobody told me."

"Your dad ought to buy a radio that works," Cull said. "Also, you never cleaned up where your horse dumped like I told you. Take this shovel and go clean up the mess."

Albert carried the shovel around back and scooped up the dried droppings beneath the mare and deposited them in a trash barrel. Luckily there was nothing fresh. When he had finished, he meandered through the store and paused in front of the candy counter. He was out of nickels. For a moment he felt like there wasn't much to live for. He went out and stuffed his papers into the double bag. Then he sat on the bag, opened a paper to the comics, and started to read.

Cull came out again and said, "It seems like you ought to get your papers delivered before midnight." The boy picked up his bulging bag and staggered around to the mare. Cull followed, saying, "Garth Hazelton got his paper while you were around back. I took mine too." The boy counted the papers again. Three short. No matter how many times he counted, he always came up with a different total. He slapped his forehead two or three times so that he would remember not to deliver extra papers to Cull and Garth.

The mare ambled around a corner into Mill Street, pausing obediently at one gate or another while the boy rolled a paper and crammed it between the pickets. It was time to make up his mind which daydream he was going to entertain himself with. Sometimes he was a Liberator pilot bombing Germany and sometimes a tank commander on Guadalcanal. Sometimes he was a cavalry officer fighting Indians and sometimes an outlaw who kidnapped Paula Ruckhart. Paula was a blond girl who had moved to town last spring. She had sat across the room from him at school and had never said hello.

He decided to kidnap Paula. At first petty distractions
got in the way of his daydream. For example, Ben Campole
was painting his eaves, and Aunt Mary Goldwin was boiling her clothes the old fashioned way in a kettle under her
elm trees. Before long Albert switched on the movie projec-
tor in his mind. He saw the outlaw tether his enormous
black horse at the church gate. A hymn came from the open
doors of the meetinghouse. When the outlaw entered, every
person turned to look. The hymn died abruptly, mouths
gaped, bodies froze. The churchgoers knew who he was because the outlaw had harried and pillaged the countryside
for months. He stopped before the pew in which the Ruckhart
family sat. "Oh, no," Mrs. Ruckhart gasped, "please, not
our Paula." Mr. Ruckhart rose half up. The outlaw waved
his rifle menacingly and Mr. Ruckhart sank feebly into his
seat. Paula emerged from the pew. Her golden hair was
fluffed into fine curls; she wore a filmy summer dress. Trembling and weeping, she looked back at her mother. Hard-
ening his heart, the outlaw gave a jerk of his head and
turned on his heel. She followed obediently. Outside he
mounted the horse and pulled Paula up behind. Although
no one inside stirred, he fired a warning shot in the air. The
horse wheeled and with clattering hooves bore the outlaw
and his clinging prize away through the streets, down a
lane, and into the junipers and sage.

On Back Street a fight between Bant and Lois Soderquist interrupted his daydream. Their screen door flew open
and Bant dashed out in his stocking feet. Lois chased close
behind, waving a stick of firewood. She wore a denim skirt
and Wellington boots. After they had circled the house twice,
Bant scrambled up a ladder that leaned against the eaves
and by sheer momentum went on up the steep roof to the
chimney. With a whimper he threw his arms around the
chimney and hugged it like a long lost brother.

Lois walked to the gate. The boy rolled a *Tribune* and
handed it to her. "The war's over," he said.

"Like hell it is," she said. "It ain't but begun." She

picked up rocks and began chucking them at Bant.

"Goldang you!" Bant roared, easing himself around to the opposite side of the chimney.

She laughed and threw harder. "He's afraid of high places," she said to Albert. Finally she took the paper and went into the house.

The boy gave the mare a lick with his belt and started on. "Hold on there," Bant shouted from the chimney. "You haven't collected yet this month. Come up here and I'll give you a dollar and a quarter."

It was an offer Albert couldn't ignore because, two months out of three, Bant failed to pay. He tied the mare to the fence, went to the door, and stuck in his head. Lois was smoking a cigarette and reading the paper. There was dust on the window sills and eggshells on the floor. "Is it all right if I go up and collect off Bant?" the boy asked.

"Jeez, yes," she said, "take anything you can get off that skinflint."

He found the roof much steeper than it looked from the ground. When he arrived at the chimney, Bant made a grab for him and Albert tumbled half down the roof before the splintering shingles stopped him. "Come on up here, feller," Bant said, again clinging to the chimney with both arms. He was a lank old cowboy who spent weeks at a time on a ranch in Nevada. His face was seamed and covered by grizzled whiskers. "Come on up here," he repeated.

"Naw," the boy said, backing down to the ladder, "I've got to get my newspapers delivered." He could see Bant was so scared that he'd grab him the way a drowning man grabs a swimmer and then they'd both roll down the roof and fall off.

The boy positioned the mare in a ditch and climbed into the saddle. At the next house he got off, tied her again, and went to the door. Mrs. Hobson, a widow who had once been his schoolteacher, answered his knock. "The war's over," he said, spreading a *Deseret News* so she could see the headlines.

She took the paper and said, "Albert, that's very thought-ful of you to call the surrender to my attention even though it's been on the radio all day. Thank God our soldiers can come home now. I suppose, of course, you've heard that poor Walt Hampstead was killed last week in training at that California airfield. They've shipped his body home. The funeral will be tomorrow morning."

"No, ma'am, I didn't hear that from anybody," Albert said. "The reason I stopped is Bant Soderquist is on his roof and doesn't know how to get down."

"My goodness," Mrs. Hobson said, coming onto her porch and gazing where he pointed. Beyond her corral and chicken coops they could see Bant on his roof, still hugging the chim-ney.

"His wife chased him there," the boy went on. "He won't let loose of the chimney. He's afraid of high places."

"That new wife of Bant's! If she isn't a scandal!" Mrs. Hobson exclaimed. "Well, come in and we'll phone some-body to come get him down."

Mrs. Hobson's old father, Simon Summerill, sat in the living room with a blanket over his legs. She had brought him from Arizona to live out his dotage. Across one cheek he had a scar as wide as a finger, which he had got in a fight with Apaches. Mrs. Hobson shouted into Simon's ear, "Father, please tell Albert a pioneer story while I phone the fire department to come get Bant Soderquist off his roof." She spoke to Albert as she left the room. "Father was one of the pioneers. You ask him to tell you a story. Get right up close and talk into his left ear."

Before Albert could say a word, old Simon began to speak, his big Adam's apple working up and down like the pump on a shotgun. "My boy Samuel lives in Salt Lake. The story he tells is that there were some fellows digging a new grave with a bulldozer in the city cemetery and they knocked open a coffin in the next grave. There wasn't any-thing in the coffin except somebody's temple clothes, which were folded up nice and neat and laid in the bottom. There wasn't a body in the coffin. Just those temple clothes folded up nice and neat. Do you know what that means? It means the Resurrection is going on all the time. That body has been resurrected. You'd find hundreds of empty coffins if you'd dig up all the graves in that cemetery."

"Now, Father, tell him how you got your scar," said Mrs. Hobson, who had returned.

"That's okay," the boy said, "I've got to get on delivering my papers."

She followed him onto the porch, and both gazed again at Bant, still huddled in a tight embrace with his chimney. Just then the siren on top of the town hall began to wail, the signal for the members of the volunteer fire department to assemble.

"They'll get him down very shortly now," Mrs. Hosbson said with satisfaction. "It was very civic minded of you, Albert, to pause in your busy schedule and seek help for him."

Albert rode up Back Street, cramming papers between pickets or giving them a toss onto porches and flagstone walks. At one place the paper skidded into irrigation water that had ponded on a lawn, and Albert had to dismount and retrieve the soggy paper. He set a dry paper on the porch and gave the railing a kick because he'd have to carry the ruined paper home and his brothers and sisters would complain that they always had to take the rejects. About that time Ralph Drayton and his hellraising buddies came roaring and weaving down Back Street in their Model A. As the car raced by, they again shouted obscenities at Albert.

While he rode up Back Street and out Cemetery Lane, Albert resumed his daydream about kidnapping Paula Ruckhart. He imagined himself and Paula in a cave concealed by thick timber. The cavern was deep and spacious and carpeted with bearskin rugs so thick and furry a person could wander around barefooted. A warm, romantic fire flickered and flamed without the slightest breath of smoke. A problem had come up, which the outlaw calmly discussed with Paula. Supplies were low and he would have to ride out to pillage and plunder. The question was whether he would have to leave her tied up. She promised she wouldn't run away. Furthermore, she cried and wrung her hands and wondered why he couldn't take her with him. For days she had wept for her mother and father and brothers and sisters, but now she was weeping for him. He led her to her bed, tucked her under a bearskin, patted her head three or four times, and vowed to return safe and sound. Strapping on his ammunition belt, he turned for a last look and she pouted her sweet little lips and blew him a kiss.

Down the lane Albert tied the mare at Sawyers' gate and knocked at the house. Mrs. Sawyer told him her husband was in the cemetery digging a grave for Walt Hampstead. Albert crossed the cattleguard behind the house and threaded his way among the graves. Rabbit bush and tall yellow bunch grass grew thick at the edge of the cemetery. Mr. Sawyer labored shoulder deep in the fresh grave. He was pudgy and bald and heaved his pick with an awkward lurch. He had suffered a collapsed lung at Pearl Harbor and had been discharged from the navy, and the church had given him a job as janitor of the meetinghouse and sexton of the cemetery.

"The war's over," the boy said, spreading out a *Tribune*.

"Too bad," the man said. "Now the bottom will drop out of the black market."

"I've come by to collect. I missed you last week."

Mr. Sawyer grasped his shovel and began to throw out gravel. Albert peered into the pit. "Mrs. Hobson's dad says the Resurrection is going on all the time," he said. "Up in Salt Lake somebody was bulldozing in the graveyard and they knocked open a coffin. There wasn't a body in it. Just temple clothes folded up nice and neat. Maybe they ought to open up Walt Hampstead's coffin. Maybe he wouldn't be in it. Maybe he would already be resurrected."

"What about my dead lung?" Mr. Sawyer grunted. "I suppose that's already been resurrected." He pulled a little

ladder into the grave and clambered out. He faced Albert.
"Look up there," he commanded, pointing to the sky. "Do
you see any angels? Look hard! Do you see any? Any at
all?"

Albert peered into the silver blue sky. "Hell, no, you
don't see any angels," Mr. Sawyer, said, setting off toward
the house.

Inside, loaves of bread smoked on the counter, and three
Sawyer girls sat at a table eating bread and honey. "Give
this boy some of that hot bread while I see if I don't have
some cash in my other pants," Mr. Sawyer said to his wife.
Albert sat at the table and slathered a fat slice of bread
with butter and honey. He took enormous bites and followed them with gulps of milk. He looked over the Sawyer
girls to see if one of them resembled Morris Hancher, because Morris Hancher was the man Mrs. Sawyer had committed adultery with while Mr. Sawyer recuperated in a
navy hospital in San Diego. Though Mrs. Sawyer had made
a public confession of her sin, she had been excommunicated. The girls were thin and freckled and had pigtails.
They didn't look like anybody but themselves.

Mr. Sawyer came from the bedroom and paid double so
that Albert wouldn't have to waste his time trying to catch
him next month. "You know why there wasn't a body in
that coffin Simon Summerill told you about?" he asked the
boy. "It wasn't because the Resurrection is going on all the
time. It was because somebody stole the body and sold it to
the university medical school. The Resurrection! My God!"

Mrs. Sawyer followed Albert from the house when he
had finished eating. She wore a faded cotton dress and had
a sad face. While the boy maneuvered his mare close to an
anthill so he could mount, Mrs. Sawyer said, "Don't you let
my husband put any bad ideas into your head. He isn't
mean to me or anybody else, but he doesn't believe in anything. You mind your daddy and mamma and you listen to
what your Sunday school teacher tells you."

"Yes, ma'am," the boy said, giving the mare a thwack.

"Thanks for the bread and honey."

He emerged from the lane and delivered along Springer Street. The mare paced briskly because they were for the moment headed toward home, and the boy slipped into his daydream. He saw the outlaw enter the grocery store. The terrified cashier clapped her hands over her mouth. Cull Stevens came from behind the meat counter carrying a cleaver. The outlaw heaved a can of condensed milk, smashing a neon clock on the wall. Cull dropped the cleaver. Turning his back contemptuously, the outlaw picked out his booty: a bottle of red hair oil for himself, a purple lipstick for Paula, a box of canned soup, half a dozen cartons of candybars, and a case of orange soda pop. He forced Cull to carry the plunder outside, roll it in a tarp, and lash it behind his saddle. The outlaw mounted, wheeled the horse about, and urged it back until its rump poised precisely before the door. There the animal obligingly did a mess. "Get a scoop and clean that up," the outlaw ordered, pointing at the stinking green pile. Then he spurred the horse lightly and cantered down the street. Mothers dashed from houses and caught up their children from lawns and sidewalks. Their worry was needless: the outlaw didn't hurt little kids.

Albert turned into Culver Street and heard a violin playing "The Last Rose of Summer." It was Osborne Wallerton, the town musician, practicing on his front porch. Wild bunch grass and yucca grew on his lot instead of lawn, garden, and trees because he lived above the ditch and was too frugal to irrigate with culinary water. When he saw the boy and the mare, the musician tucked the violin under an arm and picked his way barefooted along the gravel path to the gate.

"The war's over," Albert said.

"A solemn hush falls upon the world," Osborne replied, taking his paper.

"They're bringing Walt Hampstead home. Mr. Sawyer is digging his grave."

"So I would expect. I'm rehearsing a few pieces for his funeral."

The mare extended her neck across the aging barbed wire fence and tried to crop a strand of bunch grass. Osborne tapped her on the nose with the violin bow. As she retreated, he said, "From time to time your horse fouls my gateway."

The boy looked contrite. "She doesn't have any manners at all."

"It is the course of nature," Osborne went on. "In general the horse is a noble animal. The emperor Caligula appointed his favorite horse to be a priest, senator, and consul." Osborne scratched his heel with the point of the bow. "Poor Walt Hampstead," he mused. "He was gifted with the trombone. Now he is merely manure. But a divine manure! A vintage which the Lord hath trampled in his wrath." The mare made another pass at the bunch grass, and he tapped her again on the nose. "Mmmm," he went on, "the music for the funeral should be grand and heroic. 'The Battle Hymn of the Republic' is exactly what we need." He thrust the paper into his waist and positioned the violin under his chin. He turned and picked his way along the path, playing the piece he had named.

Abruptly he turned about, calling to Albert, "You don't intend to be a truck driver when you grow up, do you?"

The confounded boy didn't answer.

"Make something of yourself," the musician commanded, turning and again drawing his bow across his instrument.

The boy turned into West Street. At the gate of Peach Robinson's corral stood a gaunt brindle cow with large moon eyes. She seemed thirsty. Peach Robinson was notorious for neglecting livestock. The next barnyard belonged to Harold Surrey, the government trapper. Harold's battered Ford pickup stood just inside the open gate, its radiator hissing, its door hanging open. Harold stood in the back, kicking coyote carcasses out the open tailgate and shouting at his big Airedale dogs, which trotted round and round, whining and barking. While the mare pricked her ears suspiciously, the boy gazed at the tawny bodies stacked like cordwood eight or ten deep. The coyotes had crushed skulls, Harold having caught them in steel traps and finished them with a blow from a hammer.

"The war's over," Albert said, unfolding a *Deseret News.*

"By golly!" said Harold, who had been in camp. He took the paper and read. "By gum, it really is! Well, I say hooray. We shouldn't be killing people, not even if they're sons of bitches like those Germans and Japanese. All that killing isn't natural."

"They're having Walt Hampstead's funeral in the morning," Albert said. "He got killed in an airplane crash in California."

"My gosh, is that true?" Harold said in astonishment. "I'm sorry to hear it. Now isn't that terrible, isn't that just the irony of fate? An airplane crash in California!" One of the coyote carcasses which Harold had kicked out was twitching. He got a hammer from the cab and gave the coyote another blow on the skull.

"Peach Robinson's cow looks thirsty," Albert said. "Do you think it'd be all right if I let her out to the ditch?"

"You bet," Harold said.

Albert tied the mare to a post and opened the gate. The gaunt cow paced across the street, her udder swaying, and thrust her muzzle into the brown water. When she had satisfied her thirst, Albert returned her to the corral and asked Harold for a leg-up into his saddle. Seated, he said, "Mrs. Hobson's dad says the Resurrection is going on all the time. Somebody was digging in the Salt Lake graveyard and they knocked open a coffin. They couldn't find a body in it. There were some temple clothes folded up nice and neat. That means the Resurrection is going on all the time."

"A lot of tumbleweeds blow through old Simon Summerill's head!" Harold exclaimed. "He thinks he can remember whether Noah's wife was blond or brunette."

At the next intersection Albert encountered Shirley Kelsey trailing a cow which without question had just paid a visit to Layton Johnson's bull. Astride a pinto pony, Shirley wore dirty jeans and runover cowboy boots. She was very pleased to have Albert's company, telling him, "Me and dad drowned gophers today. You dig into their burrow with a shovel and clean the dirt out of the hole and you stick in the hose and turn it on. Sometimes the gophers make a dash for it and our dog gets them. It's keen!"

As they passed the movie house at the intersection of Center and Main, the mid-week matinee adjourned, and a swarm of children and a few adults came blinking out into the late afternoon sun. The cow walked among them, her back humped and her tail extended. The boy wished he was a gopher, not one that Shirley and her father had drowned, of course, but another gopher comfortably isolated in a dark tunnel. It was terrible how brazen cattle were about doing the dirty deed.

One day while Albert was eight Shirley had called him into a barn. "Do you want to play buck and doe?" she asked.

"I've got to get home," he said.

"People make babies just like a ram and a ewe," she said.

"That's nothing new. I knew that a long time ago."

"Do you want to climb up in the loft with me?" she asked. "I'll let you look at me if you'll let me look at you."

Later, after they had buckled their belts and climbed down the ladder, she said, "Don't you tell anybody." She didn't need to worry. A person couldn't have pried his mouth open with a crowbar. For two or three months he couldn't say his evening prayers. Night after night, kneeling at his bedside under his mother's watchful eye, he silently counted to a hundred and said amen.

Saying goodby to Shirley, Albert turned into Webster Street. For a minute or two he struggled to remember the lesson in Sunday school last week. The lesson might have been about Samson smiting the Philistines hip and thigh with a great slaughter or about Jesus resisting the temptation to turn stones into bread. The boy believed if he had paid closer attention to his teacher a certain rotten idea wouldn't now be roiling around inside his head like a carp in a muddy slough.

As he rode toward the cave with his booty, the outlaw had in mind that after supper he would ask Paula if she wanted to play buck and doe. Even if she didn't, he'd make her. There was no advantage in being an outlaw if he couldn't do immoral, outrageous things. When he arrived, Paula emerged and helped him unpack and carry in the stolen goods. She chattered cheerfully, obviously delighted by his safe return. He chopped wood, built up the fire, and prepared an elegant supper of macaroni and cheese and orange soda pop. He believed it a man's duty to do the cooking in camp. After supper he and Paula washed the dishes. Outside darkness had fallen; inside the fire glinted and gleamed. The outlaw felt awful. He didn't have the courage to tell Paula she had to take off her panties.

"When do I get to go home?" she asked.

"Aw, heck," the outlaw said, "you don't want to go home yet. We're just starting to have fun."

"I'm not having any fun," she said. "I'm getting bored. Sitting around this cave is worse than practicing piano all day."

"I'll tell you what," he said. "Tomorrow we'll climb into that big cottonwood in the hollow, and we'll wait until a couple of elk graze along underneath. Then we'll drop onto their backs and hang on tight to their antlers. You'll have the ride of your life."

"Gee," she said, "that'd be fun. We'll really do that?"

"You bet!"

"All right," Paula said, "I don't mind if I don't go home just yet."

Albert arrived at the gate of Ross McCrimmon, deputy sheriff. Ross pushed a mower across his lawn with his left arm because his right elbow was in a cast. His cousin Butch McCrimmon sat with legs dangling from the porch railing.

Behind Butch stood Ross's wife.

"The war's over," Albert said, unfurling a *Deseret News*. Ross stepped close, tilted his head, and stared morosely at the headline through his bifocals. Then he gave the mower another shove.

"I wonder if they'll show us those atomic bombs blowing up them Jap cities in the newsreels," Butch said. "It's too bad the war's over. Pretty soon there won't be anything interesting in the newsreels except train wrecks and hotel fires."

Butch took off a shoe and shook out a pebble. "Isn't it the truth," he went on, "that Hitler and Tojo and Mussolini should have had better sense than to get the United States into the war. They should've known we'd whip them. It's football that makes America strong. You can't whip a nation that plays football. Our soldiers are too fast."

"It was factories that beat them," Mrs. McCrimmon said. "Factories and food, tanks and ships."

"It was high school athletics," Butch insisted. "Our boys dodge too fast. They don't make an easy target."

"You never shot at an American," the deputy said. "If you had, you might think different." Ross gazed again at Albert with a long, sad face, as if he considered it wicked to smile while there were so many unpunished lawbreakers in the world. His eyes were the kind that could peer through concrete slabs. He could probably tell what a kid had been daydreaming about five minutes ago. He'd know that the outlaw had kidnapped Paula Ruckhart and had robbed Cull Stevens's store.

Though Albert hated a tattletale, he had to do something to shift Ross's attention. "Ralph Drayton has been tearing around town in his dad's Model A," he blurted. "Him and his buddies are shouting vulgar things at people."

"That Drayton kid has just barely turned fifteen," Mrs. McCrimmon said. Mrs. McCrimmon kept a census of all the underage drivers in town. Also, if somebody broke into the high school shop and stole some wrenches, she knew whose shed ought to be searched.

She went into the house and came out with a black report book. Ross had begun to mow again in his slow, awkward way. "Are you just going to let that Drayton kid terrorize the town?" she asked.

"We'll go talk to his dad and mom tonight," Ross said.

At the east end of Webster Street, Albert tied the mare to a gate and went around to the back of a tall red brick house built in pioneer times. Minerva Elverson, the spinster who owned it, rented the front and the upstairs and lived in the back. The path along the side of the house was dark with overhanging lilacs and grapevines. The boy knocked, and without a sound Miss Elverson suddenly appeared in the screen door. Her spine was curved, her cheekbones angular, her eyes haggard.

"The war's over," Albert said.

"I'm grateful," she said, "though it often seemed I had only imagined there was a war."

"I've come to collect," he said.

She opened the door and motioned him in. Unwashed dishes cluttered the kitchen table; the odor of rancid butter hung in the air. He followed her into the dim living room. Beneath a glass dome reposed a bouquet of paper pansies. She gestured him toward the sofa and took the deep chair just opposite. She rummaged in her purse and handed him a dollar and a quarter. He stood and stuffed the money into his pocket.

"Would you like fifty cents extra?" she asked, deliberately laying out two quarters on the side table. "Would you let me hold you for a minute?" she said. He didn't understand. She picked through her purse again and pulled out a bill. "A dollar," she said, "if you will sit on my lap. Just for a moment."

He pursed his lips and shook his head. She said, "Your mother has eight to hold. I don't have any." He fingered the dollar. "I had a little brother who died," she said.

"Just for a minute," he replied at last, pocketing the dollar.

dollar.

She pulled him into her lap and pressed his head against her chest. She pushed off his baseball cap and tangled her fingers in his hair. "My little one, my poor lost little one," she wept.

"I'm not lost," he insisted.

As he slid off her lap and put on his cap, she gave him the quarters as a bonus. "Please don't tell anybody," she pleaded.

"No, ma'am, I won't tell anybody in the world," he said.

Delivering along Webster, Albert was depressed. He thought he could still smell rancid butter. His spirits revived when he passed under a giant weeping willow overhanging Jerome Pindale's sidewalk. Jerome had warned the boy a half dozen times that he would take him before the justice of the peace if he caught him breaking branches from his tree. Today the door to the Pindale house was closed and the family automobile was gone. Albert couldn't resist. Standing in the stirrups, he broke off a nice switch.

He continued along Webster until he reached the Handleys' place on the edge of town. Returning, he took a shortcut across a vacant block where bunch grass and cactus grew. He decided to change his daydream from kidnapping Paula to fighting Indians because the curved willow reminded him of a cavalry saber. He gave the mare a whack. She broke into a gallop, chiefly because the soil was soft and they were headed toward home.

The major threw a glance over his shoulder, satisfying himself that his troop galloped close behind. Their mood was sober, for they understood only too well the desperate odds they faced. Yet they did not slacken or hesitate. Clearly, they preferred death to retreat. Gold buttons gleamed on blue uniforms; banners snapped in the wind; sabers stood unsheathed. In the valley before them massed a frightful horde of Indians, faces painted, heads bedecked in war bonnets, hands gripping spears and rifles. With a nod of his head the major ordered the bugler to sound the charge. "On 'em, boys!" the major shouted, standing in his stirrups and lashing his frothing stallion. The troop thundered into the wall of Indians, sabers slashing, pistols firing, lungs expelling horrendous oaths. Though the slaughter was great on either side, the day belonged to the reckless line of blue. Uttering cries of injury and shame, the Indians suddenly turned and fled. When the mare trotted into Simmons Street, Albert felt entirely satisfied. Much booty had been recovered and many captives freed. Among the captives had been Paula, who for a brief moment before the daydream evaporated had ridden behind the major, her arms securely embracing him.

Halting the mare at the intersection of Simmons and Webster, Albert counted newspapers. He could see he would be two short. While he pondered whom among his remaining subscribers to deprive of a paper, he squinted into the setting sun and saw Mr. Handley's car pull into Webster. Mr. Handley was nearly blind and drove slowly so that others on the street could take notice and get out of his way. A moment later Albert saw a Model A skid into Simmons and head in his direction; it was Ralph Drayton and his buddies. Albert knew something would happen. He reined the mare around and retreated from the intersection. For a few seconds it was a hill that blocked Ralph's view of Mr. Handley's approach; then it was the setting sun in the far end of the street. The two automobiles collided with a terrific clang. Mr. Handley's car spun about and rammed into a power pole on the corner. Ralph's car careened across Samuel Darthenspogle's lawn, bounced onto his porch, took out three roof supports, and with a great splintering of wood buried its hood in the side of his garage.

Nobody seemed injured. Mr. Handley circled his car and the power pole muttering, "Why did they put that pole in the middle of the street?" Ralph Drayton sat on the running board of his immobilized car, his chin in his hands. "That old codger," he said. "Where in damnation did he come from?" His friends picked themselves off the driveway and fled through Darthenspogle's backyard.

In a few minutes Ross McCrimmon and his wife arrived, and while the deputy asked questions of Mr. Handley, Ralph, and Albert, his wife wrote answers in the black report book. A crowd gathered. One after another, people asked Albert, who had dismounted, to tell what had happened. Among the onlookers were Paula Ruckhart and her big brother. Paula said hello to Albert in a friendly manner and listened very respectfully while he told his story. She admired the mare and stroked her shoulder and neck. The mare tried to bite Paula, whereupon Albert gave the animal a cuff on the nose.

"Oh, don't hurt the poor thing," Paula said. "She's such a pretty horse. Would you take me for a ride on her some afternoon?"

"Gosh, yes," Albert said.

After it had got dark, he said he had to finish delivering his papers. He led the mare away until he was sure Paula wouldn't see how much trouble he had mounting. As he jumped into the saddle from the fender of a parked truck, it came to him where the missing papers were. He had forgotten that Cull Stevens and Garth Hazelton had picked up papers at the store. Jogging along toward their houses, he made up his mind he'd give the soggy paper to someone besides his own family. Considering all he had been through this afternoon, he believed he had the right to lie on the rug after supper and enjoy the comics from a dry newspaper. For a little while he daydreamed that he and Paula were married and had some children and sat respectably together in church every Sunday. It made him cheerful to remember how humble Ralph Drayton had become following the car accident. It also made him cheerful to think that maybe the Resurrection was going on all the time and that maybe, if folks took the trouble the next morning to open Walt Hampstead's coffin, they'd find it empty.

THE THIRD NEPHITE

SHORTLY AFTER SUNRISE OTIS WADBY WAS DRIVING TO
work in Circleville. He stayed nights with his son in Junction, his wife having expelled him from his home in
Circleville because he had taken up with Fundamentalist
notions. She had said, "If you don't think any more of me
than to believe in polygamy, then we just as well call it
quits right now."

This morning, tense and distracted over rumors about
church trials and excommunications, Otis picked up a hitchhiker, a thing he ordinarily wouldn't have done. The hitchhiker was a runty fellow: hollow chest; scrofulous neck;
Adam's apple big as somebody's elbow; yellow mustache
running from nose to ears like a shaggy hedgerow dividing
his face into plowed, pitted properties; bleary eyes with
gummy corners. He said he was a Mormon.

"Well, then," said Otis, who was bald, stout, and be-
spectacled, "what do you make of polygamy?"

"Mmmmhmmm," the puny fellow said. "Pretty much,
yessir, that's a topic I make pretty much of. It's on my mind
night and day."

"What do you make of all the compromises with Mam-
mon and the world which the brethren have let the church
drift into?"

"It's a dirty shame. It's always been a marvel to me

how people will truckle and compromise every chance they get."

"In particular," Otis said, giving the steering wheel a belligerent shake, "what right did Wilford Woodruff and all them have to call off polygamy just because the government of the United States said they had to?"

"It's a terrible mistake to give in to the feds on anything," the little man agreed, pulling off a cowboy boot and peering into the shank. "Do so, it's just like busting your grandma's porcelain pot. You never can get it glued back the way it was before."

"You know, you ain't altogether misfavored," Otis said. "You talk a lot of sense. What's your name?"

"Name I go by in this dispensation is Simpson."

"What do you mean, 'this dispensation'?" Otis snorted. "I suppose you were around in some other dispensation."

"Well, truth is, I was." He leaned toward Otis. "I gotta be choosy who I tell this to. Take it or leave it, I'm one of the Three Nephites."

"I just imagine you are," Otis said. "You look just exactly like one of those fellows."

"I ain't telling no lie," Simpson protested. Coughing, he struck himself on the chest. "Been in Las Vegas for a while. Was stuck there, didn't know what for. Waiting my mission call, you might say. There was this big hotel fire across the street. I shinnied up one of the ladders, fought my way down some corridors, smoke everywhere, me coughing and spitting. I pried open an elevator door, climbed down the cable, hung by my knees into the cage, seen this passed out lady, knew why God had kept me in Vegas for so long. I slung her over my shoulder and clumb back up the cable. You shoulda heard the crowd roar when they saw me coming out the window onto the ladder. Danged near ruined my lungs. The smoke is what I mean."

Otis didn't say another word. He drove through Circleville and let the little lunatic out at the far edge of town. Then he drove to his own house to deliver a bundle of quilt blocks his daughter-in-law had sewed for his wife. His place was a nice rust brick bungalow with a covered porch and a carport. It seemed a shame to knock at his own door, but he didn't dare barge in.

Polly opened the door. "I was just thinking of you," she said sourly. She was short and heavy and wore a flowery print dress, ankle-high work shoes, and nylons rolled halfway down her calves.

"Viney sent you these quilt blocks," he offered.

"Well, then, give them here," she said, opening the screen door a tiny crack.

"I need to use the toilet," he said.

"Use the one in the feed store."

"It's broke."

"Use the one in the service station across the street."

"Maybe you got a leaky faucet you need fixed?" he said hopefully.

"Why aren't you ever here when I really need you?" she said. She paused. "I do have some rabbits you could look at." She came out and led him off the porch and around the house. In the back yard were six rabbit hutches.

"I can't make out whether they're bucks or does," she said.

"Well, my gad, that's easy," he replied, pushing her aside and reaching into a hutch. He pulled out a weaner rabbit and turned it upside down in the crook of his arm. Squeezing its genitals between his fingers he said, "Look there, it's kind of like a tube, ain't it? That's a buck." He seized another. "There, this one's got a kind of a furrow in it. That's a doe."

Polly was on tiptoe, peering over his arm. "Looks the same to me," she said. "There's a kid coming today to buy some."

"Get rid of these rabbits," he said. "What do you think people think of me with you keeping a bunch of rodents in the back yard?"

"Yeah," she said bitterly, "what do people think of you

slipping around preaching polygamy every chance you get. I heard they're going to cut you off the church; I heard you've been called before the high council."

"Who says I've been called before the high council?" he said indignantly. "Seems like I'd know about it if it was so."

She squinted at the sun. "Don't get in my way," she said. "I've gotta dig carrots." She rummaged in the toolshed for a shovel and entered the garden. She stamped and pried with the shovel, her breasts heaving, her arms quivering.

Otis dangled a sheaf of carrots by the tops and knocked off dirt with a stick. "You know, you're sure something nice. You're as sweet as a package of M & M's. I'm moving back in. I'm so lonesome I'm just dang near dead. I wake up in the middle of the night and I got nobody to rub up against."

"No way are you moving back in," she said.

"Ain't you just a little tiny bit lonesome for me, sweetie?"

"It's too late. They're going to cut you off and then we're finished for sure."

Otis came close and she smashed a clod and looked away toward the neighbor's corral. He put his arms around her from behind, although because of her buttocks and his belly his hands came short of clasping. "You wouldn't let a man have just a little grazing in the pasture, would you — a man that's been starving for weeks and weeks?"

"If you'd give up those silly ideas," she said.

"Just a little romp, just this morning. There ain't no need to tell anybody else about it."

"Get your hands off my breasts."

"They're so nice," he said.

"You aren't going to graze in my pasture," she said. "Never again."

He drove to the feed store on Main Street, which he and his brother Angus had inherited from their father. He was astonished to see the runty hitchhiker trundling a wheelbarrow full of digging tools around the corner of the store. "I been hired to dig out your sewer line," Simpson explained. "Seems your toilet don't work."

Inside Otis accosted Angus, who stood behind the service counter scrutinizing sales slips. Angus wore bib overalls and his thick gray hair sprouted backward like grass bending in a heavy wind.

"That waterskeeter thinks he's one of the Three Nephites," Otis said.

"I don't care if he thinks he's King Solomon," Angus replied. "He can dig, can't he? I'm getting tired of running across the street to the service station every time I need to relieve myself."

It being Angus's month to manage things, Simpson continued picking and shoveling and Otis went fuming back to the office. A two-by-six plank, set on edge, divided the office; the brothers had ordered it installed after their falling out over Otis's Fundamentalist ideas. There was a roll-top desk on either side. On Otis's side were shelves lined with religious books — *Precious Truths Cast Away, Awake, Zion!, The Errant Keys: Where Does Latter-Day Authority Truly Lie?*, and so on. In a corner on Angus's side, hanging by its neck from the ceiling, was an effigy, a life-sized, straw-stuffed replica of Connor Stuart, Otis's Fundamentalist friend. "That son of a bitch has led you astray, and I just want you to know what I'd do with him if I was king of this county," Angus said the day he tied a gallows knot in a rope and strung up the effigy.

Otis shuffled papers, trying to concentrate on invoices for rock salt and cattlegrub medications. From time to time he glanced respectfully toward the effigy hanging in the corner, which in an odd way did look like Connor Stuart, having hooked eyebrows and a shaggy mustache scribbled in black crayon on a flour-sack face. Nobody deserved worship more than Connor. When the stake president had summoned him for trial, he hadn't backed down an inch on the revelations he had received.

Otis closed the office door in order to have a talk with the effigy, he of course serving as mouthpiece for both parties. "So," he said for Connor, "you went over to your own house and laid your hands on your wife and got steamed up and lustful. About one more minute and you would've sold me out just so you could go into your bedroom and do what the animals do."

"The spirit is willing but the flesh is weak," Otis mumbled.

"Just tell me this," Connor demanded. "Is it an honor or dishonor to be excommunicated from a church that has fallen into apostasy?"

"Oh, it's an honor, a real honor."

"Then answer me this. Do I have the Holy Ghost or don't I?"

"That you do! You've got him, no question about it. Your telephone dials direct to God. It's you who's got the keys to this dispensation."

"Well, now, I never personally made no such claim about the keys," Connor said modestly. "All I said was somebody somewhere has got them and it sure ain't the president of the church."

"I'm going to do something big and get myself excommunicated," Otis promised. "I'll quit sneaking around and lying low. I'll come right out into the open and preach from the rooftops."

Leaving the office, Otis gave the effigy a brotherly pat on the shoulder. In the mill behind the feedstore he helped Lester, the hired hand, mix and sack a batch of chicken mash. Otis stacked while Lester filled and sewed. As he deposited each sack, Otis gave it an impolite bump, imagining it was Polly, who deserved a little shaking up. "You think it tickles me to think about marrying another wife, don't you?" he said bitterly to a sack clutched in his arms. "You think I'm an old ram that's still in rut. Dammit, Polly, it ain't so. If God told us we couldn't be saved in any other way, if he said we couldn't know our election was sure without living a celestial law of marriage, who are you and me to raise the puny arm of flesh and say no?"

Around ten o'clock he returned to the service counter to

inventory the chicken mash. As he entered the room, voices died abruptly. Angus labored over a sales slip for Sarmantha Kinch, who tapped her car keys on the counter. Cauley Wexler and Jerald Garfront leaned against the counter, both studying the progress of a spider down a dangling light cord. Simpson, taking a break, lounged red faced and sweaty in the front doorway, tippling from a bottle of strawberry pop.

"Well, hell," said Cauley, who was an outsider, "why are we all standing around with a finger in our nose? Why worry about telling the truth? Otis, I'm proud of you. I don't care what you believe, anybody who stands up to the church, by gosh, I respect that man."

Angus reamed an ear with the eraser of his pencil, saying grimly, "Congratulations, brother, you've finally went and done it."

"Done what?"

"Got yourself called up before the high council."

"What liar says I been called up? Seems like I'd know about it, don't it?"

Jerald had stepped back from the counter. "I never meant to pass no stories along. I just heard it happened."

Sarmantha, close to eighty, patted her pile of gray hair, from which old-fashioned horn combs rose like pitchforks from a haycock. "All I got to say, Otis, is there's a great sorrow on the Other Side. Your poor father and mother watching down from heaven above while you deny the Prophet and make light of the promises you made in the holy temple! That poor wife of yours! Thirty-seven years she's waited on you hand and foot and this is the thanks you give her."

Simpson swallowed the last of his pop and belched. "Now I'd conjecture you was married in the St. George temple," he said. "I know some things about that temple which would boggle your mind. You'd think they was impossible. For instance, did you know the rafters ain't held together by nails nor wood pegs nor rawhide binding, just by the power of the priesthood? Chew on that a minute.

Just the magnetic force of the priesthood keeps them tim-
bers together."

"That is the damnedest story I ever heard in my whole
life," Otis said.

"You been in the attic of the St. George temple?"

"No and you ain't neither."

"I've been places might surprise you," Simpson said,
tapping his nostril three or four times.

"Is that really so about those rafters?" Sarmantha asked.

"Yes, ma'am," Simpson affirmed, "it's really so."

Otis walked down the street for the mail, knowing he
couldn't do another thing until he saw whether he had a
summons. He said good morning to the postmaster, and while
he dialed the combination of his box he whistled as if he
hadn't a worry in the world. There was nothing except orders, bills, and advertisements. He felt wobbly and weak as
he returned to the feed store, and he took a drink of milk
from the refrigerator in the storage room. He went out back
to the mill and helped Lester sack a batch of rolled barley
mixed with molasses and vitamins for cows. He threw the
sacks down with contempt, once in a while giving one a
kick. He imagined each one was Cyrus Lambert, the stake
president, with whom he was grappling in mortal combat.
"Cyrus, you pig bladder," he said, "quit playing cat and
mouse with me. If you're going to cut me off, well, go on,
get it over with. I can't take this waiting."

By and by he looked up to see Simpson in the doorway.
The little man had flaring jaws but hardly any chin at
all, as if a contractor had graded a nice, smooth cut-and-
fill between his Adam's apple and nose and had set up
his bristling yellow mustache as a drift fence to keep
sand dunes off the roadway. When Lester had shut off the
mixer, Simpson said, "I come back to apologize. My big
mouth has run away with me. Look, ain't it a monster?"
He opened as wide as a hippopotamus's mouth and pointed
down his gullet with a finger. "How can a fellow with a
mouth like that keep from offending people? He can't,

that's all there is to it."

"That's all right," Otis said. "Water breaks out of everybody's headgates once in a while."

"I was wondering about an advance so I could buy some lunch."

"That's Angus's department."

"I looked around. Can't seem to find him."

"Likely you've got some good in you," Otis said. "Answer me straight. Do you want to bust out of that story book you have been living in? Do you want to give up the lies and untruths that has been swarming around in your head like flies in a pigpen?"

"Absolutely! You better believe it!" Simpson cried.

"All right, I'll just test you. I'll take you to lunch where you can get some education."

They climbed into Otis's car and drove across town to Connor Stuart's place. Fronting the street was a large building of prefabricated metal where Connor's men serviced and repaired the diesel trucks and semis he hired out around the state. Behind was a double mobile home where lunch was in progress. Connor's first wife, Geraldine, let Otis and Simpson in. Connor waved a hand and went on eating. Also at the table were his new wife, his mechanic, and one of his drivers. The newcomers pulled up chairs as Geraldine set two more places. Otis served himself some green beans mixed with bacon bits and passed the dish to Simpson.

"Oh, boy!" Simpson said, ladling out four or five spoonfuls.

"Might be somebody else would like a little," Otis said.

"Oh, there's plenty," Geraldine assured. "Try some of this meat loaf."

Cindy, Connor's new wife, put down her knife and fork, looking as if she wanted to be helpful but didn't know how. She was Connor's secretary and dispatcher: nylons and half high heels, blouse with tucks, hair nicely curled, eyes shadowed, a fine looking young woman. Nobody would have said that about Geraldine, who had bow legs, wispy yellow hair, lips that could never quite close over protuberant teeth.

Lunch progressed quietly. Geraldine spoke briefly about the signs of the times. The driver asked Cindy about a truck that was on the road. The mechanic asked Connor for his opinions on dove hunting. "One dove makes no more than a mouthful," Connor said. "It's like making a meal on hummingbird tongues."

Connor had thick brown hair, a honed knife-blade nose, a black bushy mustache. He buttered a crust, spread a little marmalade, then pushed the dish down the table to his guests, saying, "So where are you from, Mr. Simpson?"

"More or less from Las Vegas. Last station of duty, you might say," the little man replied, cheerfully slathering his bread with marmalade.

"From Sodom and Gomorrah," said Connor.

"Yessir, that is correct. A sewage pond, that's what Las Vegas is. One night I seen a murder about to happen. Down the alley behind the Vegas Greyhound station I seen a man about to take off another. Had a .357 magnum pressed to his temple. I says, Hold on there, you son of Cain, this is salvation speaking; hold on there and God'll shortly assist you by killing the mangy dog with a disease. Victim looked syphilitic, to be truthful. I saved this feller from a life sentence. Talked him out of his gun and sent him home resolved to look for a job come Monday morning."

"Now you've ate, your mouth has got big again," Otis said.

"Geraldine, pass Otis some of that nutcake," Connor said. "How's the wife? I haven't seen her in some time."

"Hard-hearted as ever," Otis said.

"I wish I could talk to Polly," Geraldine said. "Maybe I oughta look her up. I saw her day before yesterday in the mercantile, but you know how things are there, everybody watching like a hawk."

"Don't fret yourself over Polly," Connor said. "No water's going to come out of that well." He took a toothpick from a dish in the center of the table. "The rumor I hear is Otis has been called up. I wish it was true."

"I went down to the post office to see if I had a letter," Otis protested. "There wasn't any. That Cyrus, he's playing cat and mouse with me."

"Hogwash!" Connor said. "He's got no reason to excommunicate you. It takes somebody valiant to merit excommunication."

A flush came up Otis's neck. Connor reached for his hand. "I just wish you were willing to go up to Golgotha with me."

The mechanic said, "I'm sure standing by you."

"Otis is going to stand by me too," Connor said. "God wants you to make a move, Otis. He wants you to take another wife. Then you'll get that letter."

"I just ain't had the courage."

"It's Sister Marva God wants you to take."

"Can't he find me a prettier one?" Otis lamented, rolling his eyes toward Cindy.

"A pound of pretty isn't worth an ounce of dung," Connor said. He turned to Cindy. "He's got a deep spirit, that Otis, but he doesn't know everything there is to know. He's got celestial marriage and worldly marriage all mixed up. Go on, sweetheart, tell him how it is between you and me."

Cindy stared at her plate and mumbled, "I couldn't."

"I'll tell him," Connor burst out. "She says she isn't ready for a baby yet. So I say no carnal knowledge then. When she's ready, I'm ready. Till then we sleep together for a test. There, that's what celestial marriage is like. You take that Sister Marva, Otis. I've already had a discussion with her. I've said, Otis will be coming around, count on it. Go take her, brother."

Connor motioned toward a bookshelf. "Now to other matters. Get me the scriptures," he said to Geraldine. To the right of his plate he laid out the Bible, in front the Doctrine and Covenants, to the left the Book of Mormon. "Mr. Simpson," he said, "Otis has brought you to this table to hear the word of the Lord. I hope your heart is receptive."

"Yessir," said Simpson, "I'm one of the most receptive fellows I know."

Connor fixed his eyes upon the little man and began, his voice accelerating until his words were whirling thick and fast. He bobbed, grimaced, pointed, and chopped, saying, "Back in the days of President John Taylor when he and two thirds of the apostles were on the underground and the church was in receivership to the federal government and the gates of hell were open wide and the winds of evil blew unto the furthermost corners of the earth, President Taylor, speaking to a small assembly in Bountiful, prophesied that the day the church caved in under the pressures of its enemies and foreswore and annulled the sacred principle of celestial marriage, on that very day it would cease to be the one and only true church of God Almighty and would be no more than an excrement upon the face of the earth, a mess of vomit regurgitated out of the bellies of Moloch and Baal." Simpson fidgeted with a button on his shirt, one eye squinted, his nose wrinkled. As for Otis, he followed every word with great concentration, fearful that some little sound or meaning might escape him. Admiration ran through him like millet through a sluice, and he vowed to repent of his pusillanimous ways.

When at last Connor had finished, Simpson said, "I'm very favorable toward all them ideas. I recall one time being in a bar in Missoula, Montana, and a big feller, drunker than a skunk, actually, which by the way, I would like to make a comment on the character of that city, which a whole lot of people don't appreciate enough . . . "

"Hold up there, you prevaricator!" Otis shouted. "Ain't you got no respect for the truth when you hear it? This runty rascal thinks he's one of the Three Nephites. He can tell you more lies in two minutes than you and me could think up in a month."

"Well, now, I ain't no prevaricator," Simpson insisted. "You take it or leave it, it don't make no difference to me, because I certainly wouldn't of brought this matter up in the present company, but now that you mention it, the truth is I am one of the Three Nephites."

Otis rose and seized him by the shoulder. "No more of that wormy talk, you weasel."

"Sit down," commanded Connor. "Let's hear him a little."

Simpson glared at Otis. "You're lucky I don't thrash you. I may be one of the Three Nephites, but that don't mean I don't have a temper. I'm going to tell you a sacred, heart-rending story even if you won't believe it. I was there when Moroni buried the Plates. By gad, that's the absolute truth. Me and him seen the destruction of the Nephite armies by the Lamanites. Oh, it would've wrung your soul with the very dregs of bitterness to see them armies dwindling, battalion by battalion, platoon by platoon. When it was just him and me, hiding in the trees, him digging a hole in the hillside for them Gold Plates, he said, Crithee-ahhad — that was my true Nephite name — Crithee-ahhad, I hope you can reconnect with them other two Nephites that get to wander the earth till the Lord comes again, because it's going to be hell for lonesome if you can't. And I says . . . "

"Heavenly Father, strengthen me," Otis said, stamping from the house with a slam of the door. He circled his car ten or twenty times before he calmed down enough to sit behind the wheel. Shortly he heard thumping inside. The door burst open and Simpson leapt out and crashed to the ground.

Connor and the mechanic stood on the porch. "He's possessed of an evil spirit," Connor said, wiping his hands on his pant legs. "It isn't him talking in his own true personality. It's a clever demon. Hank and I are willing to lay on hands for casting it out, but if he's going to fight, let him sink into the infernal pit where he belongs."

"Amen," said Otis, "I'm all for that."

Having returned to the feed store, Otis performed some bookkeeping at his desk for an hour or two. He had a hard time entering figures into the calculator because his mind was on Marva Brinkerheisly, whom even a sex fiend wouldn't have thought of molesting. She was a spinster school teacher of thirty-five or forty, an enormous, gaunt woman who perpetually resembled an elk in the late stages of malnutrition. Otis could see how polygamy worked. When a man was young and randy, God let him choose among tasty, appealing women like Polly. Later God called him to accommodate the leftovers and wallflowers who had as much right to exaltation as anybody else.

Hoping that God wouldn't think he was like Jonah, balking over his call to Nineveh, Otis retired to a storage room for prayer. He knelt in a crevice between an old unused stove and a stack of bagged oats. "Oh, God," he prayed, "kindly send me a sign that I'm supposed to marry Sister Marva Brinkerheisly—a big, sharp, unmistakable sign, if you please. It seems to me she's a little over the hill when it comes to having babies. And me too, Heavenly Father—I'm not sure I've got what it takes to raise up a posterity with her. However, all things are possible with you. Amen."

Suddenly there was a terrific noise in the stove pipe, a descending clamor of scratching and flapping. Something thumped into the pit of the stove and wings beat against its walls. "Who's there?" Otis cried. From the stove came more flapping and fluttering. Then he choked with gratitude. "It has to be a dove!" he gasped. "A dove, a sure sign of confirmation. Oh, thank you, Lord, thank you!"

He jerked open the stove door and out tumbled a magpie. The black and white bird fluttered upside down on the floor, then revived and with a squawk shot toward a high bright window. It struck the glass, bounced, and spiraled to rest upon a sack, lying at a cant, its breast panting, its beak open.

Otis seized the bird whereupon it clamped upon the flesh between his thumb and forefinger. Roaring, he dashed through the storage room, through the office, past the service counter where Angus looked up with open-mouthed surprise, and out of doors, where he heaved the bird into the air. With another triumphant squawk it launched into flight.

"Oh my gad," said Simpson, who stood at the corner of the building with an air rifle in his hands. A boy stood beside him. "I was just showing him how to adjust this gun for windage," Simpson explained in a mollifying tone. "There's them magpies in your elm around where I'm digging. I sure didn't think that crazy thing would loop down your chimney. However, it's good to see it ain't hurt any." He handed the rifle to the boy. "Here, sonny, maybe you oughta light out for home."

Otis walked around and peered into the trench Simpson had dug along the foundation. The little man pointed at an opened pipe. "Right there is where the roots was clogging your sewer. Won't be long and you can enjoy your toilet again."

"I want you to know something, Mr. Simpson," Otis said. "If it was suddenly my turn to manage this feedstore, I'd fire you in two seconds."

"You'd be exactly right. I'd fire me too if I was in any position to do so. In the meantime, I'll try not to knock any more trash down that chimney."

A little later Otis helped Lester sack a batch of horse pellets. When it was his turn to stack, he hugged the hundred pound bags with great tenderness, supposing they were Marva. Looks in a woman weren't so important. It was a sweet temperament that counted. He imagined the ways he would charm Marva, also the ways she might charm him in return. "Here," he said to her, seated at the breakfast table, "have a little sugar on your germade, also some of this cream," whereupon she said, "You're so gallant." Then they were no longer at the breakfast table but in the bedroom, whereupon Marva didn't look like herself but like Dolly Parton, in whose blond tresses and pillowy breasts Otis buried himself.

In the late afternoon, tending the service counter, Otis saw school children straggling toward home. "Heavenly

Father," he said under his breath, "if Marva will just be somewhere that I can talk to her without anybody hindering, I'll take it as a sign that you have ordained this marriage."

He drove to the elementary school and, having circled through deserted halls, put his head into Marva's room and found it empty. He went out the back door and saw her far across the playing field taking down a volleyball net. He said, "I had in mind a place that wasn't quite so public, Lord." Then, remembering Jonah, who had ended up in the belly of a whale, he added, "Sorry, Lord, you know best."

He strode across the grass, meeting Marva in the middle of the field. She towered over him, the net bunched in the crook of her arm. Her bony shoulders filled out her blue serge dress like springbars in a tent; a gold and amethyst brooch clung to the leveled plains of her chest. She said, "If you're looking for Mr. Smollit so you can apply for the janitor's job, he's probably in his office."

"I was thinking maybe I could do some janitoring for you."

She bit her lip and with hands suddenly atremble shook out a portion of the net and tried to bunch it more neatly.

"Here, let's fold it up proper," Otis said, taking the trailing end and stepping away.

"Oh, yes," she said, "that would be so very helpful."

When they had folded it, Otis said, "Now I'll just carry it for you."

"Oh, you don't need to do that, Brother Wadby."

"I just might call you Marva and you might just call me Otis," he said. "What do you think of Otis for a name? There was a German prince named Otis. The first Otis we know about in our line came to Philadelphia in 1872."

"My gracious, the antiquity of your family!" she said.

He said, "I'll sure have to watch my language around you, you being a school teacher and knowing the pretty things that oughta be said."

"No, not at all, I like men who use bad grammar. It seems they'd know what had to be done in an emergency."

"I do have to say I've got a knack for getting things done. If the mill busts down, I don't shilly-shally around. I get on the phone and get a part ordered two minutes later. Sometimes I've jumped in my car and made it up and back from Salt Lake with the piece we need the same day it busted."

"I'm sure you do have a knack for getting things done," Marva agreed. "I just know you do."

From a distance they heard shouting, then barking, then more shouting. A large gray dog suddenly careened around the corner of the schoolhouse and loped across the playing field. A rod or so from the couple the animal halted. Someone had recently trimmed its body, leaving ribbons of hair dangling from its ears and a wiry mane circling its neck. In its mouth was a rubber doll. It began to bark belligerently, its great deep voice muffled by the doll, which it seemed intent upon retaining.

A man, wildly waving a shovel, broke around the corner of the schoolhouse. It was Simpson. The dog resumed its flight. "Stop that vandal!" the little man shouted. Arriving beside Otis and Marva, puffing and heaving and greatly vexed, he cried, "Why didn't you grab him while you had a chance?"

"Who had a chance?" Otis protested.

"Dogs are the bane of civilization," Simpson expostulated. "They bark all night, bite strangers, and befoul sidewalks with dung. There was this family from California gassing up at the station across the street and the little gal's doll fell out and that puke of a dog snatched it up and made off. The little gal squalled and hollered, of course. I says to myself, maybe right here is the reason God sent me to this stiff-necked, ungrateful town; maybe getting this doll back is exactly what I'm supposed to do. It ain't just a question of making that little girl happy. You gotta consider the public relations angle too. What's it going to do to the tourist industry if everybody in this city just sets back and lets depredations like this go on unchecked?"

The dog, having been turned back by the woven wire fence at the edge of the schoolyard, now made a furious dash past the three persons. With a wild flourish of his shovel, Simpson chased after the animal, shouting, "Hyyarr, you offal-eating rascal, come back here."

"You talk about depredations!" Otis said to Marva. "It seems like to me that fellow is a bigger liability to this town than a hundred dogs."

Back at the feed store Otis tended the service counter for a final hour after Angus and Lester had gone home. He brooded on the ability of one misbegotten soul like Simpson to frustrate the plans of the Almighty as they related to Otis and Marva. Still he wouldn't concur with Connor's claim that the runty fellow was possessed of an evil spirit. It would be a pretty poor specimen of an evil spirit that would trifle with a person as unfavored as Simpson.

Soon the bell over the outside door jingled and Polly came in. "I need ten pounds of rabbit pellets," she said.

As he weighed the pellets in the storage room, Otis had a little chat with the scales, which he imagined were Polly. "Now, honey, you know I wouldn't of gone to see Sister Brinkerheisley if I hadn't been called of God to do so. That's the absolute truth, sure as I'm alive."

The scales said, "What you was called of was your male appendages, you billy goat."

As he handed Polly the parcel of pellets, Otis said, "If I was home I sure as hell would talk you into getting rid of them rabbits."

"Well, you aren't home," she said, "so I guess I'll keep them. I sold three of those weaners to the Jorson kid this afternoon. Two does and one buck. He's getting into the breeding business."

"You sure they was two does and one buck?"

"I told him they were according to my best light. However, I said if time proved otherwise he could bring any or all of them back and I'd replaced them with some others."

Otis followed her onto the steps and watched her walk down the street. She had rolled up her nylons and put on her Sunday flats and touched up the little circle of curls around her head. He could have cried, she looked so nice.

At dusk he locked the store and headed for Junction. All day he had been as taut as barbed wire on a new fence, but now, as the car picked up speed, he began to relax. Then ahead he saw a man thumbing at the side of the road. Sure enough, it was Simpson. Otis pressed the accelerator and raced by. In the rearview mirror he saw Simpson shake a fist. Suddenly, a couple of hundred yards beyond, a front tire blew out with a boom and the car lurched from side to side. As Otis wrestled it to a halt, the shredded tire emitted a loud thunk, thunk, thunk, thunk. Climbing out, he saw Simpson jogging toward him. He grabbed rocks and began heaving, shouting, "Back off, you loony, stay your distance!"

About thirty yards from the car, Simpson paused, scratched his head, and squatted, watching in the dusk while Otis placed the spare tire on the wheel. "You know," he called, "if I could get up a little closer, there's some things I could tell that you'd give plenty to know about."

"You get any closer and I'll brain you with this jack handle."

"You ain't exactly being hospitable," Simpson yelled. "Seems like to me I done you some good favors today."

"Favors! You coyote! I can't remember a worse day since the time that horse fell on me when I was a kid." Otis grunted and tugged, working as fast as he could.

Finally Simpson rose and shouted, "I better warn you, I'm getting mad. I'm getting ready to dust off my feet on you."

Otis pounded on the hub cap, gathered his tools, and threw them clattering into the trunk.

"Listen, you mealy-mouthed pervert," Simpson hollered. "You just dirtied on your last chance for salvation, that's what you done. The Lord sent me this way to kick you out of your orbit around that pestiferous, piratical Connor Stuart. Are you grateful? Not by a damn sight. You're surly, mean, and peevish. Come Judgment Day, God's going to wipe his hindpart with you and flush you down a toilet and I say good riddance of bad rubbish."

Otis stood with his mouth agape. Suddenly he couldn't see Simpson. He took a step or two, blinked, stared again. The runty man had disappeared. On either side of the road were open fields, low wire fences, dry, shallow ditches — no hiding places whatsoever. Otis trotted down the road, paced back and forth where Simpson had been. "Merciful heavens, he's gone!" he said.

His hands trembled until he could hardly insert the key into the ignition. Once the engine had started, he turned the car around and sped back to Circleville. He went into the feed store, stacked his Fundamentalist books on his desk, then sat and dialed the telephone. "Marva," he said, "Sister Brinkerheisly, that is to say, this is Otis Wadby. Forgive me for my wicked intentions. I came over there this afternoon to propose that you and me get married. Probably you wouldn't of had me which would have been just exactly right. You're the finest woman there ever was, but I'm all locked up. I'm going home to Polly."

Then he got on a chair and unnoosed the effigy which had dangled in the corner for six months. He carried the limp, straw-filled body into a darkened storage room, where he laid it tenderly on a stack of wheat. "Connor," he said, "the reason you didn't have any luck casting an evil spirit out of that scrawny, emaciated little boar is he really is one of the Three Nephites." He could hear Connor's indignant protest. "I know he don't look like one," Otis replied. "Furthermore, he's foul mouthed and dissipated. But when it came to the big act, I swear it's true, I seen him do it. He evaporated into thin air — poof, in the twinkling of an eye he was gone." Otis stroked the effigy's head and fingered its shirt collar. He said, "I can't go along with you, Connor. It seemed like to me I could see the Holy Ghost standing right behind you, but I still can't go along."

He drove to his house and went up the steps. He hesitated only a moment, then went in without knocking. Polly was at the kitchen sink, finishing her supper dishes. He deposited his books on the dining table and sat down. "I'm back to stay," he said. "I've given up on Fundamentalism."

She watched with an open mouth while he leafed through the volumes. "This one," he said, hefting *The Errant Keys: Where Does Latter-Day Authority Truly Lie?*, "is one very fine book."

He went outside, she following. He threw the books into the incinerator barrel, doused them with gasoline, and set them afire. Lighted by the dancing flames, he and she stood awhile. "Don't cry," she said, brushing his cheek with her fingers. "We oughta be awful happy, hadn't we?"

"About them rabbits you sold that Jorson boy," he said. "Tomorrow I'll go over and check them out so we can get him squared away with what he needs."

"Do you want a little supper?" she asked.

"It seems like it's an unholy thing to do just now," he said, "but I'm danged near dead for lack of a romp."

"Well, then it's a romp we'll have," she said. "I'll fix you some supper later."

PETROGLYPHS

HUMPHREY COLBORN, A DOCTORAL CANDIDATE IN history at the University of Utah, lived with his wife and daughters in married student housing. He was city-bred whereas Connie, his wife, was a country girl. For several years, a dismantled bicycle and a greasy hibachi sat on the landing opposite their apartment door. He never discovered to whom they belonged. At last Connie sold them to a neighbor for six dollars. Humphrey respected her initiative in practical matters but lamented her indifference to the improvement of her mind. He often felt he had married beneath himself.

He planned to write his dissertation under the direction of a historian of the English Renaissance named Harriet Cullen, with whom he had a remarkable affinity. A sinewy woman of sixty, Harriet said it was her purpose to mold Humphrey into the world's foremost authority on the wool trade between the Cotswolds and Flanders during the reign of Elizabeth I. She coached him to an outstanding performance on his preliminary examinations and negotiated a grant whereby he could accompany her to England for research.

On a Saturday evening shortly before Humphrey left for England, he and Connie went to a party at Harriet's house. Upstairs and down the plushly carpeted domicile swarmed with professors, students, and their friends. The young couple found the buffet, loaded their plates, and took refuge in the den. There they were greeted by Harriet's husband, Preston, who asked whether they had examined his collection of canned corn labels. "Please meet Mr. Zoraguchi, our horticulturist," Preston said of his Japanese gardener, who wore a dark double-breasted suit. "And this is Miss Murray, our boarder," he said of a robust young woman who sat on his other side. Miss Murray, thought to be reliable because she was a Mormon, received board and room and a small stipend in return for providing a circumspect companionship to Preston on evenings and weekends when Harriet was away. Owing to heart disease, Preston's once-large frame had shrunk and his lips were a perpetual blue.

Humphrey soon wandered from the den and joined a group who had been shooting arrows at a target on the back lawn. Among them were Harriet and an art professor named Dillis. The latter, a loquacious, theatrical person, was describing last year's hot air balloon regatta at Park City. "I'll swear," Dillis said, "there was this one balloon, sewn in a bifurcated way and bizarrely colored, I assure you, and it looked for all the world like an upside down scrotum. Exactly like a giant, floating scrotum!"

Dillis took notice of Humphrey. "Where's your wife?" he said. "Left her home, I suppose. Tired of her already. Marriage is a dreadful business, anyhow." He peered into Humphrey's glass. "Soda!" he said with disgust. "You Mormons are so fastidious. Harriet, send this boy in to the bar for something with fiber. Pour him a mug of stout. Stout, I say, dark as floodwater, warm as urine."

"Don't pick on him," Harriet said. "Everyone to their own taste."

Instantly he lost interest in Humphrey and, turning to others, took up what seemed the thread of an earlier conversation. "Hieronymous Bosch was one of the few who had a clear eye in the Renaissance."

"Bosch was medieval and so are you," Harriet said.

"Not medieval, universal rather," Dillis insisted. "Take his painting, 'Garden of Delights,' the greatest painting of all time. 'Garden of Delights' eddies with grotesquerie. A cavalcade of nudes astride wild animals circle a pond. A man gnaws at a strawberry big as a beach ball. Another thrusts flower stems into the backside of a kneeling fellow. A pig dressed in a nun's habit makes love to a man. Seated on a stilt-legged chair, a purple monster devours human beings, stuffing them into a beetle-beak one at a time and defecating them in great purple bubbles through a hole in the bottom of the chair, whence they drop into damnation."

"Bosch was a reactionary, a canker in the root of the Renaissance," Harriet said.

"Harriet really believes in all that twaddle about the great revival of learning. Unfortunately she infects her students with it." Dillis placed a hand on Humphrey's shoulder. "From kindergarten through grad school, you've leaped the hurdles, dived through flaming hoops. What for? Just so you can someday strut and posture in front of students, mouthing weighty verities no one can understand. All your life you've nursed the secret conviction that you're extraordinary, that you're destined to mighty works and a brilliant career. Well, you're not. Go home, you dolt. Give up your illusions of academic grandeur. Work in a bank. Mow your lawn, tend to your irises."

"If I can be a professor, that's all I'll ask," Humphrey said. "I've never counted on being famous."

At that moment, Professor Turmainder, the chief inebriate of the history department, appeared upon the patio dressed only in his undershirt and boxer shorts. "Would you give me a hand?" Harriet asked Humphrey. Together they steered the frail professor into the house, down a hall, and into a spare bedroom, where they tucked him into bed. "Now go to sleep," Harriet said, tenderly smoothing her colleague's unruly hair.

"Please don't pay any attention to Dillis," she said to Humphrey, who stood on the other side of the bed. "He doesn't mean anything personal. He's irascible but not petty. He'll insult you one moment and give you a hundred dollars the next. He's far more moody than he likes to show. They've crucified him in the art department. They've denied him his promotion again. It's affected his self-esteem terribly. I tell him no matter what he mustn't stop work on his Picasso book, but he's very gloomy."

Humphrey knew Harriet and Dillis went to coffee every school-day morning. Certain graduate students claimed they were lovers, a rumor Humphrey refused to believe. Dillis was too dour, too obscene, Harriet too devoted to her ailing husband, too rational and magnanimous, too committed to the academic quest. Moreover, she was ten years his senior.

In the hall Humphrey and Harriet met Connie. "We've just got Professor Turmainder to sleep," he explained, feeling very unlucky to be found emerging from a bedroom with Harriet. "He was running around in his underwear."

"I saw him," Connie said. "He took off his clothes at the last party too."

"Do you want to go home now?"

"If you don't mind. You can stay and I'll come back and get you."

He decided for diplomatic reasons to go with her. While they adjusted their seat belts, she said, "I felt like a cat at a dog show in there."

He gestured impatiently. "They'd like you if you'd give them half a chance. Why didn't you circulate a little?"

"What would I say?"

"You could talk about the news. Everybody in the world watches TV. I could suggest some topics of conversation if you'd let me prep you a little. For example, you could talk about the Tour de France with Professor Stohler. Dr. Brannor likes to talk about his cabin at Island Park."

"I don't think I can ever get used to parties like that. I'd much rather go to a party at church. But I'll try harder next time. Please help me remember about Dr. Brannor's cabin."

"They're not bad people," Humphrey said. "Not even Dr. Turmainder. He's a sweet old man who has an addiction. They are all educable people. Their sins are the sins of not knowing."

Much later that evening, after they had gone to bed, she snuggled against him and said, "I'm sorry I made you come home from the party early. Every minute I'm at one of those parties, I'm sad. I think, These are the people Humphrey sees every day, these are the people he wants to be like, these are the people he loves. I admit I'm jealous. If Harriet was any younger, I'd be scared to death."

"That's silly!" he said.

"It's going to be very lonely when you're gone to England."

"I'll think about you and the girls every day. I'll write you every night."

"Make love to me now," she said. "Do it the old way. Stay inside like you used to do before we decided we shouldn't have any more babies for a while."

"My gosh!" he groaned. It was he, rather than Connie, who had been reluctant to use contraceptive devices. For a moment he resisted her request, listening to the breathing of their daughters, who shared the bedroom. Lena, four, slept on a narrow cot; Helen, one and a half, slept in a crib she had almost outgrown.

Connie had begun to weep. "Half the time when those airplanes crash, they don't know who's really in the coffins because everyone gets burned beyond recognition."

"The airplane won't crash," he insisted. He obviously had to pay whatever ransom she might exact before releasing him to depart for England. He kissed her hand, her wet lashes, her soft, relenting lips and found himself suddenly wanting her. They made love; she held him tightly upon her body, murmuring over and over, "I do love you so awfully much." He too loved her inordinately yet at this moment wished he didn't. He often fancied there was such a thing as a pure and disembodied love. He had been assured there was by the Renaissance writer Castiglione. Once he had persuaded Connie to read a passage from Castiglione. She had shrugged her shoulders and said, "If we're not supposed to love each other with our bodies, why do we have them?" She was a congenial but simple woman.

Humphrey and Harriet stayed three days in London, where she gave him an orientation to the repositories of Tudor manuscripts and shipping records. On their last evening in the metropolis, they had a quiet dinner in their hotel restaurant. There were candles, starched *serviettes*, delicious broiled chops served with mint sauce. Staring thoughtfully at her wine glass, Harriet discoursed on the Renaissance origins of the Enlightenment of the eighteenth century.

In his room Humphrey suffered an ecstatic insomnia for hours. He penned a letter home, grieving that he had only the uncomprehending Connie with whom to share his volcanic emotions. "Forgive me for being so happy," he wrote. "It is a happiness that makes me love you all the more. I have never before realized so clearly how each of us must have his own renaissance, his own revival of learning. We are born again through knowledge. Please do not be jealous over Harriet. She is a marvelously moral and upright person."

The next day Harriet and Humphrey drove in a rented car to Cirencester, where they took quarters in the Lyonnaise, a small inn of French pretensions. After they had rested, they called on Miss Priscilla Throckmorton, a gaunt, red-haired spinster who lived in a renovated grange on the edge of town. In Tudor and Stuart times, Miss Throckmorton's ancestors had owned a manor in the Cotswolds; their tenure as the squires of that manor, Trullydon, was the topic of Humphrey's dissertation.

"So Mr. Colborn is the young man who will resurrect my dead grandfathers," Miss Throckmorton said cheerfully. She handed Humphrey a whiskey and water, from which he took the slightest sip. They sat on a patio shaded by an ivied arbor.

"He's a very able scholar," Harriet said. "His wife comes from a sheep ranch in southern Utah, so he knows a lot about sheep culture."

"Then the rustic offerings of Cirencester won't seem so unbearable," Miss Throckmorton said. "There's to be a performance of 'Hugh the Drover,' an opera you might call it, by the Choral Society, assisted of course by the Grammar School Choir. You and Harriet must come as my guests."

"I'm sure it'll be very professionally done," Humphrey said.

"It would be quite redeeming," she went on, "if you could assure me the Americans are sometimes contrite over their impetuous Revolution. Don't they sometimes wish they were still Englishmen?"

"Gosh!" Humphrey said. "No, I never heard of anyone being contrite over that. Still it does seem a shame to have fallen out of sorts with our mother country."

"Yes, very much a pity. But now look at the bird in the ivy there. I believe it's a female preparing to make a nest. Tell me whether our sparrow has taken over America as we are often told it has."

"There are plenty of English sparrows," Humphrey said. "It never occurred to me they actually came from England."

"There you are! It's good we've lent you something besides a corrupt version of our language. A rich race, the Americans. On the whole, insensitive, I believe. Brutal, really. Exploiters and militarists. Having their nukes, as one calls them, they lord it over the rest of the world. It's they who'll start World War III. And it's us, poor Brits, who'll be at the epicenter of the devastation."

"Oh, dear," Harriet said, "I hope you're wrong. If it's of any comfort, we sleep as insecurely as you. On the day of Armageddon you'll have your revenge. The tidal wave of destruction will spread from the center and inundate us as well."

The next day the three drove into the Cotswolds in the rented car. In time their winding road led to the farmstead called Trullydon, at present owned by a London solicitor and farmed by a hired farmer, Mr. Huggin, who invited his guests into the imposing farm house for tea. The farmer and his wife were a ruddy-faced pair from Lancashire. "Me and the missus are permitted a bit of profit-taking on the side," he explained. "Our chief cash crop isn't corn or stock as you might think, but her Majesty's subjects on holiday, knocking on the door inquiring for bed and breakfast." In time the conversation turned to sheep. "Oh, wot animals won't do!" Mrs. Huggin averred. Her father had owned a ram named Whiskers, which she pronounced Weskus. The ram butted neighbors, boarded buses, and more than once emitted a malicious shower of pellets on the parsonage doorstep. " 'e knew wot 'e was doing, no question of it."

After tea Mr. Huggin accompanied his guests outdoors, where the sun had broken through a lowering sky. They climbed the slope behind the house and surveyed the farmstead. On the hillsides were pastures enclosed by walls of unmortared stone and grazed by cattle and newly shorn sheep; in the valley bottom were fields of wheat. Miss Throckmorton unrolled an aerial photograph of the valley for Humphrey's orientation, it being among his tasks to create a map of the manor as it had existed soon after James Throckmorton, an obscure burgess of Bristol grown wealthy in the brokerage of wool, had purchased it in 1546. It was possible, Miss Throckmorton admitted, that the most exacting perusal of the court rolls, deeds, and charters in the municipal offices of Cirencester would not reveal the pattern of cottages, arable strips, and unfenced commons buried beneath the existing fields of wheat.

"I'm afraid you'll have to resort to some digging," she said to Humphrey. "Mr. Huggin, would you kindly show Mr. Colborn where the spades are kept?"

"She's takin' you on," Mr. Huggin reassured the startled Humphrey. "She's a wry one, the mum is. Don't pay 'er no mind."

Miss Throckmorton took Humphrey's arm while they

descended the hill. Her nose was long and uneven; her teeth discolored and capped with gold. "I must warn you about a certain ancestral uncle of mine named Peter," she said. "He was vicar of Cirencester in the later reign of Elizabeth, and his parishioners brought an unsuccessful action for his removal for the preaching of nonconformist doctrines. During the disturbances of 1596, he allowed himself to mix with a Puritan mob against Lord Fancheverell, who was attempting to execute a commission of array in Cirencester. A soldier pierced Peter's cheek with a pike, and the cheek healed imperfectly. It was a kind of second mouth, you might say, from which air whistled when he preached with passion. For that reason he became famous, during his later years, as the Trumpet of Cirencester."

Harriet said, "It's a marvel he wasn't hanged, or at least left to rot in prison, for having resisted Her Majesty's officer."

"I wouldn't know the reasons for his lucky escape," said Miss Throckmorton. "I for one could live rather easily with the fact of his hanging, had it occurred. Please, Mr. Colborn, if you'll promise not to mention a word of him in your dissertation, I'll invite you to tea every afternoon. You can't imagine what scones my Mattie makes, which she serves with Brittany jam."

In his letter to Connie that night, Humphrey described Miss Throckmorton and her errant predecessor, the Trumpet of Cirencester. "It appears I am to be bought off from telling Peter's story by tea and scones. It will be very unscrupulous of me to have a daily cup of tea. You don't suppose I'll become addicted, do you? I'm sure you'd love Miss Throckmorton at once. She never cracks a smile, yet is joking at every moment. Luckily I have Harriet to keep me from making too big a fool of myself."

For a while Humphrey was very happy. Each morning he had an early breakfast with Harriet at the Lyonnaise. After breakfast, Harriet drove to Bristol for the day, where she researched bills of lading in the archives of the Port

Authority. Humphrey, remaining in Cirencester, made pho-
tocopies of the account books in which Miss Throckmorton's
ancestors had recorded the hiring of servants and the pur-
chase of land, livestock, and goods. That task completed,
he moved to the Municipal Offices, where he examined legal
records, entirely in Latin, for land transactions relating to
Trullydon. He anticipated each new fact with pleasure; with
equal pleasure he took tea with Miss Throckmorton every
afternoon and at night had dinner with Harriet following
her return from Bristol.

Some ten days before the end of their stay, Humphrey's
savor for England disappeared. Thereafter, the ubiquitous
clouds, through which the sun broke perhaps two or three
times a day, oppressed him, and the houses of Cirencester
no longer seemed charmingly antique but cramped and dirty.
His disillusionment began one evening when he returned to
the Lyonnaise to find Dillis Rowbury, Harriet's friend from
the art department, who had supposedly been in Barcelona
researching his book on Picasso.

Dillis was a slight, lean man with curly hair, furrowed
cheeks, and scowling lips. He had arrived in Madrid, he
explained to Humphrey, intending to proceed to Barcelona.
However, while loitering in the Prado he had undergone a
marvelous epiphany. His distaste for the academic regimen
had welled up powerfully, and with a sudden motion of
mind he had liberated himself. Instead of going to Barcelona,
he had redirected his travels to France, Holland, and Germany. Now, out of money, he had come home to Harriet.

"I'm through forever with that prick, Picasso," he said.
"I'm dropping off the academic treadmill. No more entering exhibitions; no more pretense about writing a book. They
can't fire me. I've got tenure."

The two men took dinner without Harriet, who had not
arrived from Bristol. Afterward they retreated to the bar, a
mere cubicle, where, against Humphrey's objection, Dillis
poured Humphrey a mug of stout. "I really shook her up,"
Dillis said of Harriet. "When I phoned her, she said, 'You

can't drop Picasso.' I said, 'It's done, it's over with, I've dropped him forever.' So she said, 'Well then you'll be getting your ass back to Utah on the first flight out; I'll take a day off and put you on the plane!' Jesus, I love that woman. As the poet says, 'There is a garden in her face, Where roses and white lilies grow.' But when Harriet wants to be bitchy, she outclasses Nero's mother. Sending me back! My God, that's what I call infidelity."

Befuddled from a few sips of stout, Humphrey went to bed before Harriet arrived. He heard voices in the hall and the closing of her door and knew she had taken Dillis in for the night. Lying in the dark, he waited for that particular creak of the floor or elevation of a voice that might tell him they were making love; he prayed that when it came he would have the fortitude to burst from his bed, pound on the wall, and with indignant shouts denounce their shameless adultery. At last he slept.

Harriet and Dillis joined him at breakfast. Harriet intended to get an early start for London where she wanted Dillis to see some Renaissance sketches before she put him on a plane. Dillis, looking haggard, swilled coffee and took little else. "Keep working as usual," Harriet instructed Humphrey. "I'll be back tomorrow night."

She returned the next evening in time for dinner. She drank a half-bottle of wine with her salmon and leeks. "Dillis is over Greenland by now," she said to Humphrey, glancing at her watch. Then, with astonishing candor she recounted Dillis's recent activities on the Continent. In the vicinity of Pont St. Michel in Paris he had encountered a genuine old-time mountebank, a traveling pantomimist who paused in public places to demonstrate his ability to ingest whole cigarettes and unsheathed razor blades, a deception, of course, a prestidigitation of the mouth and gullet. Dillis fell in with him, and they traveled to Amsterdam, Brussels, and Frankfurt, where they regaled themselves in bistros and bars and houses of prostitution.

"He's unconcerned about the possibility of having exposed himself to AIDS," Harriet concluded. "He assures me he very carefully used condoms in all crucial encounters. Furthermore, he has a curious sense that his visitations among the stews and brothels of the Continent do not amount to infidelity. He is mystified why I should be offended since, as he claims, he preserved his undeviating love for me in an unsullied corner of his heart."

Harriet became so unsteady from the wine that Humphrey had to help her up the stairs. At her door she leaned against his breast and said, "You mustn't think I'm disloyal. I have always admired my husband very much. No one was more clever, no one more authentically ingenious than Preston. I feel fierce and violent whenever I think of anyone hurting him. I'd do anything to protect him."

She slipped her arms about Humphrey's waist and began to weep. "The issue of course is what I must do about Dillis. I've never before held a wake over a living person. Dillis is so pathologically cynical. He pretends to be nauseated by his own mediocrity. But it seemed so wonderful, so rejuvenating, to fall in love with him. For once in my life I did something impulsive. It's been hell watching him deteriorate. My God, I can't have two invalids on my hands! Life can't be that unfair! I made up my mind the Picasso book would be the test. I couldn't believe it when I got his call in Bristol day before yesterday. Till just now I haven't been able to admit it really is the end."

She released him and stood back. "Well, I must brace up. Thank you for letting me tell you. You're such a good friend." She entered her room and closed the door.

He sat in his unlighted room for a long time, wrestling with an impulse to flee the inn. His body still felt her heaving, incestuous ribs. He couldn't assimilate, he couldn't fathom, the stark impropriety of her having held him so tightly. He couldn't guess whether it was an adultery or a rape. As the dark hours dragged by, he recognized the complexity of his anguish. The goddess he had worshipped had evaporated in an English mist. This woman, Harriet Cullen, had fallen long ago from the grace of the ideal scholar. Like an unschooled wench, she milled in the thickets of carnal love. And with that fact duly registered, he began to see that knowledge didn't bless, but injured; it didn't enlighten, but merely disabused.

On the night of his return to Salt Lake City, Humphrey made cautious, unsatisfying love to Connie, who, he was relieved to learn, wasn't pregnant. A couple of days later he returned to campus where Harriet proudly installed him in the commodious office of an absent colleague. For a few days he worked on a map of Trullydon, assigning tenants to particular plots and distinguishing between plowed land and pasture; then he turned his attention to the narrative of Trullydon's squires.

One morning Dillis dropped in dressed for tennis. Though Humphrey fidgeted, Dillis was in no hurry. Thumping a bare knee with his racquet, he discoursed on his passion for paleolithic art, conceived when he had visited the caves of Lascaux in France. In time, Harriet appeared and the two departed. After their game, Harriet returned alone to Humphrey's office, still clad in a tiny white skirt and sleeveless blouse. Her sleek, moist hair was tied in back.

"I know Dillis kept you from work," she said. "I'm afraid it's my fault he stayed so long. I didn't want to break in and take him away to the tennis court any sooner. You're so healthy and cheerful and unruined. You can't help but be good for him."

"I didn't mind at all," Humphrey lied.

"Obviously I haven't been able to disentangle myself from Dillis. He isn't up to the shock of separation. When I returned, I found he'd been steadily drunk from the day I put him on the plane at Heathrow. He has to be let down easy. I'm sure he has better prospects than I represent. I simply have to be clever enough to help him discover them." As she left, she gave Humphrey's shoulder a squeeze. "You're truly a dear," she said.

Thereafter Dillis appeared at about the same hour every day, passing time until Harriet was ready for tennis. Humphrey's sense of crisis grew until at last, shopping one evening with Connie and the girls, he felt he had to confide his disillusionment to his wife. While he pondered a way of bringing up the matter, he entertained his daughters, who sat in shopping carts, with whimsical charades.

Holding up a bottle of green detergent, he said, "This is a giant green-bellied pike. It swims this way and that. It is a voracious predator. It is very hungry. What shall we feed it?"

Giggling, Lena pointed toward a bar of soap. "Ah, yes," Humphrey went on, taking up the bar, "this is white-scale chub. It is a bottom feeder. It likes to swim lazily in warm waters. It belongs to an overabundant species. It is happy to be a link in the great ecological chain. It likes to be dinner for the giant green-bellied pike, which at this very moment lurks here amidst these reeds, heating its frying pan and setting its table."

Connie shortly asked him to calculate the price per ounce of toothpaste. "They keep changing the prices," she complained. "Sometimes the little tubes are a better bargain than the big ones."

When he had pocketed his tiny calculator, he said to Connie, "Speaking of pikes and chubs, I feel I'm being eaten alive these days. I've found out a terrible thing about Harriet. She's been having an affair with that art professor named Dillis. He showed up one night in Cirencester and she took him in. You can't believe the rotten things he did in France and Germany. Now she wants to break up with him but doesn't know how. She's afraid he'll stay drunk night and day."

"Do you mean a real affair?" said Connie. "Are they sleeping together?"

"A real affair is exactly what I mean. They've been rank and loamy with one another. She claims they aren't sleeping together now, but that's irrelevant. She still spends a lot of time with him. It's ugly any way you look at it. All this time her husband has been telling everyone how he appreciates her great devotion. Poor Preston! He's a cuckold, a gull, an unwitting dupe."

"That's terrible," Connie agreed. "But you shouldn't be too surprised. A lot of people behave that way."

"Dillis comes to my office every morning and wastes my time. Then Harriet comes in and says, 'Thanks, Humphrey, you're so wonderful, putting up with poor lonely Dillis.' I hate him. His mouth is dirty as a sewer. I wish she'd dump him and be done with it. I'm a friction pad between them. They're grinding me to pieces."

They pushed their shopping carts into the dairy aisle. Humphrey took Helen in his arms while Connie selected skim milk and eggs. "Harriet has got into the habit of telling me all kinds of things I don't want to know," he said. "On the flight home she filled me in on the history of feminine hygiene before the twentieth century."

"She's a brassy woman," Connie said. "I don't imagine anything would embarrass her."

"I'm trapped. There's no way to move out of that office. She's too pleased with herself for having got it for me. No other graduate student has one like it. I can't afford to offend her. She has to pass on my dissertation. Till I've got my degree, I'm a prisoner and she's my warden."

At home Connie put away the groceries while Humphrey gave the girls a snack and tucked them into bed. He turned out the bedroom light and sang lullabies until they fell asleep. When he returned to the kitchen, Connie sat at the table. He sat opposite her and she pushed a small package before him. He took it up and saw it contained condoms.

"I put it into the cart," she confessed, "after you took the girls out to the car."

"You're very forward," he said. "I couldn't stand to have a cashier see me buy these things."

"I don't suppose you're in the mood tonight," she said glumly. "You haven't been yourself ever since you got back from England. We made love the night you got back and never since. Now I know why."

"These condoms won't help. They'll just complicate things. I hate to give in to passion. I try to refrain as long as I can."

"I know. You've got lots of self-control. But I'm frightened of Harriet. She doesn't believe in God. What does she care about the commandments? She's used to getting what she wants, and now she's through with Dillis she'll go for you."

"That's silly," he said. "She's sixty years old. Moreover, she really wouldn't be interested in me. I'm just a timid bookworm. My nose is big and I wear frayed collars. When I laugh, it's like water going down a drain."

"You don't laugh very often," Connie said. "I like to hear it when you do. I think you look awfully nice. Lots of women tell me you look nice. I feel lucky you'd want me for your wife. But if days and days go by and you don't want to make love, I wonder what's wrong with me. If you don't want to make love to me, then pretty soon you'll want to make love to somebody else."

"What a sordid situation!" he said. He picked up the condom package and read the fine print. He opened it and removed a foil container. "If I must I must, I suppose. But I couldn't do it in the bedroom anymore. Not with the girls sleeping there."

"We could do it on the sofa."

She turned out the light and drew him from his chair. She hugged him, then began to unbutton his shirt. It struck him as bold, promiscuous, to begin without taking a shower and putting on pajamas and gown. She unbuckled his belt and his pants dropped, and she slid a hand down his inner thighs. Admitting he wanted her indecently much, he mourned, for a final, fleeting instant, the human propensity for wantonness. She unfastened her bra and drew his hands over her breasts, murmuring, "Please don't feel guilty. It's me who has to be your mistress. Nobody else."

At the office nothing changed until the next week when Harriet asked Humphrey to accompany her to Dillis's apartment. For only a moment Humphrey fancied himself strong enough to say no. Driving along South Temple, Harriet spoke of the inadvisability of returning to a scene so symbolic of her former intimacy with Dillis; she went only because she hoped, by visiting his studio, to steer his latest initiative in painting toward a beneficial end. Pursuing his interest in primitive art, Dillis had recently been doing simple abstractions of mammoths, saber-toothed tigers, and other extinct animals. Unfortunately he had conceived a fantastic notion of painting one of these animals on a sheltered cliff somewhere in the wilds of southern Utah. He intended this image to appear authentically old. He would paint it among authentic prehistoric petroglyphs, using charcoal and ochre which an archeologist friend had found in the midden heap of an Anasazi ruin.

"Wouldn't that be a forgery?" Humphrey said.

"Yes, of course," said Harriet, "you could call it a deliberate fraud. As he describes it, it would be a satirical gesture, a joke on the academic world he despises so much. I doubt anyone would be really taken in by it, at least not anyone who counts. I confess it's the idea of defacing a cliff that troubles me. I hate to see wilderness violated in any manner. He's pressing me to come along on a backpack trip, but I've told him he'll have to carry out his grotesque little project without my assistance."

Dillis's living room was a gallery of exotica. On opposite walls hung an African war shield and a hairy Polynesian fetish; dominating a corner was a stuffed orangutan, not taken from the wild, as Dillis was quick to explain, but delivered to the taxidermist following its demise in a zoo. At its feet lay a climbing harness and belaying rope. "The tackle is mine, not the ape's," Dillis said. "I have become a serious rock climber this summer. I'm proud to say I've a good deal of talent for it."

They went down a dim hall toward his studio. A bedroom door stood open. An abstract design decorated the bed cover; a fresh white columbine stood in a vase on the night stand. Harriet gave Dillis an accusing glance and went by. He stood fast and called her name. She turned and waited.

"Send this open-mouthed Humphrey away so we can talk," he commanded. "Look at him stare, calf that he is. Give him the keys to your car and let him go back to campus."

"Please be civil to Humphrey," she said with exasperation. "I'm the one who insisted he come."

"I'm aware of that fact," he said. He threw his hands into the air. "Can't you relent? Can't you have mercy? How long do I have to do penance? I wasn't myself during those feverish days on the continent. I've steadied myself, Harriet, I've sincerely repented. Won't you please stop insisting we're the best of friends. We're not friends, we're lovers."

"We can't possibly discuss this topic in these circumstances," she said. "I can't think clearly at all. I want to see your studio. I want to see these animals you're painting on rock."

"Send him away," Dillis pleaded. "He doesn't want to be here. I'll cook you a splendid lunch, and we'll sit in the studio with a glass of wine. I've got ideas, I've got plans. Stay awhile and let me fill you in."

"I haven't time for lunch," she said, "I've things I mustn't fail to get done. I want to see your studio and then we're going."

He brushed angrily past her, saying, "*Que ce soit comme tu veux.*" He opened the door and bowed elaborately. "*Madame, monsieur, veuillez entrer de toute manière, s'il vous plaît.*"

A skylight lit the studio. In one corner rested a heap of sandstone slabs, in another, a row of mortars and pestles for grinding powder. In the center stood a sturdy easel bearing a sandstone slab. On the stone a rhinoceros had been painted with charcoal and ochre, mere lines and shadings giving remarkable shape to a shaggy creature with a horn on its snout.

"You've done it!" Harriet said delightedly. "It's perfect. It couldn't be better."

Dillis pursed his lips skeptically. As far as technique was concerned, he said, the painting was nothing. Its virtue, if it had any, lay in its mockery of the humbuggery and affectation which characterized the world of art and scholarship. It was this figure that he planned to duplicate among the petroglyphs of a cliff in southern Utah. Perhaps he would paint it on several cliffs. Toward that end he had been making himself adept at rock climbing. He intended to rappel from the cliff top in order to lead later observers to the conclusion that the painting had been done in ancient times before erosion had lowered the soil at the base of the cliff.

While Dillis spoke, Humphrey seethed. He felt obliged to protest even though his thumping heart might rupture in the attempt. He yearned for the equanimity of Socrates and Sir Thomas More in the face of death. "But you couldn't sign your painting if you put it on a cliff," he finally objected. "It wouldn't mean a thing if you couldn't sign it. Nobody would know it was yours."

"Sign it! What do you take me for? An egoist? A sycophant to fame? A toady, a lickspittle? None of that sham and hypocrisy for me, none of the posturing and politicking. These days it isn't talent that makes a painter; it's promotion, it's hype and PR."

Humphrey wrung his hands. "But mighn't it mislead somebody? Mightn't someone think it's authentic?"

"Naturally someone will think it's authentic!" Dillis roared. "That's the point. If you hear the rumor that Dillis Rowberry has run out of creativity, if you encounter the slanderous notion that he never had any to begin with, give it the lie. Here is my magnum opus, my *chef-d'oeuvre*. Because of it I'll be known to after generations as the anonymous master of the Utah canyons. I'll take my place among the great primitive artists of the world. I'll enter the fraternity of Lascaux and Altamira."

"You can't be serious," Harriet said.

"Of course I'm not serious!" he cried, turning on her. "If Humphrey asks a stupid question, I give him a stupid answer."

"I mean serious about painting the rhinoceros on a cliff."

"Ah, there, Harriet, I am serious, deadly serious."

"I was afraid you were," she said.

At noon the next day, Harriet stopped Humphrey outside his office door, saying that as a result of a long phone conversation with Dillis she had reversed her position on the proposed forgery. "It isn't a very big image which he plans to paint, no larger, really, than the one we saw on his easel. It can't greatly disfigure an entire cliff. You could even argue that it'll harmonize with its wild environment, perhaps even enhance it. I know it's a crazy scheme, but it seems to have taken on an almost mystical significance with Dillis. I'm half persuaded it really might serve to vent all this anger he feels against academic formality; it might really allow him to turn his thoughts to something more productive."

At that moment Professor Turmainder, who was teaching summer session, shuffled by, giving them an affable greeting. "He's under discipline from the dean," Harriet said after her stooped colleague had entered his office. "Students complain of his being drunk while grading exams. We have to do something to help him."

"But that's a problem for another day," she went on. "For the moment, I've got Dillis to worry about. I've agreed to go along on the backpack trip. He refuses to go without me. He's like a child who wants to show his mother he's learned to ride a bicycle. It won't be the first pack trip we've had together. However, I told him it couldn't be we two alone this time. The condition of my coming along is that you come too. He objected of course. So I put it very categorically. I reminded him that you're infallibly discreet. I know it's a great imposition on your time, but I really don't know who else to ask. I don't think you'll find it unpleasant. An amble into wilderness might be precisely the refreshing break you need."

She paused for his consent. His heart again thumping with anxiety, Humphrey fidgeted with a tape dispenser and said nothing.

"You won't let Harriet down?" she pleaded. "You will come along, won't you?"

"If you need me, I'll just have to come along," he blurted. "I wouldn't want to let you down."

After she left, he sat dumbly before his computer for hours. From mid-afternoon he roamed the campus, ending at the university bookstore, in whose calm, nearly deserted interior he found a temporary relief. At one stand he leafed through Newton's *Principia Mathematicae*; at another, he examined sermons by a Mormon apostle; at yet another, he studied a handbook on lesbian love. "It's closing time," said a winsome girl, who flourished a feather duster. He wondered whether she had read the handbook on lesbian love. The murderous anarchy that reigned among books, the brutal competition between ideas, came upon him, as did the pathetic naivete of Milton's famous declaration, "Let Truth and Falsehood grapple; who ever knew Truth put to the worse in a free and open encounter?" Of itself, he was thinking, knowledge had no moral force; knowledge could only empower the corrupt human will to greater evil.

That night a small fan stirred the stifling heat of his bedroom. For hours he listened to the rhythmical breathing of Connie and the girls. When at last cool air eddied through the window, he nudged Connie awake.

"Harriet insists that I come on a pack trip with her and Dillis," he said. "I didn't have the guts to say no. Dillis won't like it at all. He'll be rude to me every second of the trip. Maybe he'll push me off a cliff or chop me to pieces with an ax."

"My gosh!" Connie said. She padded into the kitchen and got a drink of water. He followed and, while they sat in their nightwear at the table, he explained Dillis's plan to paint a forgery upon a remote cliff.

"He hopes to hoodwink the archeologists and scholars of primitive art," Humphrey said. "He thinks that would be very funny."

"I think it'd be kind of funny too," Connie said.

"It isn't funny. It's terribly immoral. Not that I ever expected anything better of Dillis. It's just like him to create a hoax. It's Harriet who disillusions me. At first she said it'd be wrong because it would deface a wild cliff. Now she says we'd better humor Dillis; it'd be a wonderful therapy for him and what's a little painting in the middle of a big, wide wilderness?"

"If you don't like it, don't have anything to do with it," Connie said. "You don't have to go on that pack trip. If you can't say no to Harriet, let me do it for you."

"I can say no," he said, his fingers drumming the table top. "I see very clearly now what I must do. I'm dropping out of my Ph.D. program."

"That's no way to say no!"

"It is," he insisted. "I've looked at the situation from every angle and there's no alternative. I don't want to be a professor anymore. It hurts too much to see that professors are just as dishonest and malicious as everybody else. They of all people should know better. I don't want to be around them. I'm dropping out."

"Don't say that. You're almost through. Just hang on one more year, and you can get an appointment and move away from this mess."

"My mind's made up. I'm not going to the office tomorrow. I'm sitting here without a single doubt. I feel marvelous! All of a sudden there's a monstrous burden off my back. I've been in school since I was six years old. I've been a galley slave for twenty-one years."

"Oh, jeez," she said limply, "what'll become of us now?"

He slept late in the morning and had a leisurely breakfast with Connie and the girls. His mood of liberation continuing, he borrowed a neighbor's paper and read the hiring ads. After lunch he went to the zoo with Connie and the girls on money his mother had sent for Lena's birthday. At the sea lion pool, he rejoiced in the freedom of the frolicking smooth-skinned seals. In the feline building he pitied the relentless pacing of the large caged cats and congratulated himself upon his own escape from bondage. However, standing upon a high walkway in the giraffe house, he suffered a change of mood. While Connie assisted the girls at a machine which molded plastic toys, he gazed upon a gigantic male giraffe. The animal was a gothic marvel. Its cloven hooves were bases, its enormous front legs columns, its neck a tower, its knobby pate a gargoyle, its back, descending into stunted rear quarters, a flying buttress. All of this, combined with the animal's sad eyes and delicate muzzle, reminded Humphrey of himself, who during twenty-one years of schooling had hidden his head amidst a high foliage of illusory information. A terrible loneliness came over him, and he began to weep.

The girls came running, showing their toy giraffes and demanding to go on to the hippopotamus house. He allowed each to grasp a hand and lead him to the door, where Connie waited. Though he averted his face, she saw his grief and said, "Poor Humphrey, you do feel so bad, don't you?"

"Never to be a professor! This is a terrible, terrible day, the worst of my entire life. All at once I've been turned upside down. No, it's worse than that. It's as if suddenly one of my legs is gone or both my arms. I can't imagine what on earth I'll do to earn a living. There's nothing else I want to be."

She wiped his cheeks with her fingers. "It breaks my heart to see you cry. Who gave that awful woman the right to trample us into the mire? I say let's stay in this rodeo. You go back to your office tomorrow. You tell Harriet you stayed home today with a touch of flu. Work as hard as you can. Do whatever she says with that stupid dissertation. Just get it done. I'll wheel the girls to campus every day with your lunch. If I need to come oftener, I will. I'll stick my head into Harriet's office and say hello bright and cheery to remind her you're already taken. I'll chat with her about anything you tell me to. If she thinks she's going to steal pigs out of my pen, she's got another think coming."

"I can't face them any more. I don't have the nerve. I can't possibly go on that pack trip."

"Of course you can go. I'm coming too. I promise I won't let them hurt you."

Harriet came by several days later while Humphrey and Connie had lunch with their daughters on the campus lawn. When she mentioned the pack trip, Connie said she'd like to come along too. "By all means you must come!" Harriet said. "I'm ashamed I didn't think to invite you from the start." Connie described petroglyphs in a canyon thirty or forty miles from her parents' ranch and said they might drive within hiking distance of them in her father's four-wheel-drive pickup.

"What would it take," Harriet asked, "to inveigle an invitation to inspect your father's sheep operation? Might your parents host us overnight?"

"You wouldn't want to see it," said Humphrey. "It's a very small ranch and it's awfully cluttered by worn-out equipment."

"Why wouldn't she'd want to see it?" Connie protested. "What does it hurt if there are a few old trucks and balers kicking around? Everybody else's ranch looks the same."

The campers departed on a Friday morning in Harriet's van, bringing along Lena and Helen to stay with their grandparents at the ranch. A minor scene ensued when Dillis emerged from his apartment without his paints and climbing gear. "This damned trip isn't mine," he growled at Humphrey after Harriet had persuaded him to return for his equipment. "The only reason I'm going along on this fool's errand is to keep an eye on you and Harriet."

"It wasn't my idea," Humphrey said. "I'd much rather stay home."

At a service station Dillis bought root beer for the girls. "Look at these deprived little turds guzzle that pop," he said. "I doubt they get much else than oatmeal and broccoli at home."

"I'd like to murder him," Humphrey said to Connie before they resumed their seats in the van.

"Keep your cool," she said. "Let me do the talking."

When they arrived, Connie's mother ushered them into her living room. She had waxed the scarred hardwood floor and cleaned the bearskin rug. An oval-framed photograph of Connie's grandfather hung on a wall. On another wall were antlers holding a lever action rifle and a shotgun. "Jesus," Dillis breathed, "these people are the real thing. You don't make them any more authentic than this."

In the late afternoon Connie's father took them into the mountains to inspect his sheep herd. They found the herder, a shy young Ute, smoking a hand-made cigarette in the door of a camp wagon. His saddled horse was tied to the wagon tongue, and two border collies panted in the shade of a nearby aspen. Nearly a thousand ewes and lambs grazed on a steep opposite slope, a wooly roil amidst yellowed grass and white-trunked aspens.

"Though you may not be able to tell it," Connie said to Harriet, "the sheep are grazing in a planned direction. Tomorrow they'll be over the ridge into the next canyon. The herder takes advantage of slope and cover to steer a herd the way he wants to go."

That night the girls slept on pads in their grandparents' bedroom. As honored guests Harriet and Dillis were assigned the other bedrooms, while Humphrey and Connie were exiled to a spare camp wagon in the barnyard. "I'm sorry," Humphrey said to Connie while they undressed, "but your parents' home always smells musty. I knew very well we shouldn't bring Harriet and Dillis to the ranch."

"It doesn't smell musty," Connie said. "Besides, what's

so wonderful about Harriet and Dillis? She's a weasel and he's a skunk."

The next morning Dillis was again in a rebellious mood. After watching the others load their backpack gear into the four-wheel-drive pickup, he announced his own refusal to follow suit. "I see no purpose in going a step farther on this misbegotten camping trip. I already feel a blockage of my creative process. I can't paint in front of gawking peasants, for God's sake."

"Oh, dear," Harriet said, "I was hoping we could have a pleasant outing. You've battered me for weeks to accompany you to a wild cliff where you could paint your rhinoceros. I've arranged this trip at a considerable inconvenience to myself and, I might add, to Humphrey and Connie, who are guiding us to a cliff abounding with the petroglyphs you wanted."

"What is this talk about a rhinoceros?" Connie demanded. "You didn't tell me he meant to paint graffiti on my cliff. I didn't know that was what he wanted to do. He can't do that. I won't allow it."

"Won't allow it!" cried Dillis. He fetched his pack from the van, tossed it into the back of the pickup, and climbed in beside it. "Onward, fellow campers," he called. "I for one find a renewed interest in this expedition."

Connie raised the hood and checked the oil. "Why did you cross him?" Humphrey grumbled. "We could've gone home early."

"I'm looking forward to sleeping out," she said. "Besides, Mom'd be disappointed if we took the girls home ahead of time."

A couple of hours later Connie parked the pickup, and they cinched on backpacks and entered a tributary canyon. In places the canyon narrowed till its sheer rock walls were scarcely five yards apart; in other places it widened into pleasant alcoves of sagebrush and willow, checkered with sun and shadow. After several hours, the hikers saw a lizard of an extraordinary upright posture. Like a miniature tyran-

nosaurus rex, it had strong hind legs, tiny forelimbs, and
ferocious eyes. Dillis got on his knees before the crevice into
which it had dashed and fumbled with his camera. Mouth
agape, the lizard charged out.

"Drive it back!" Dillis shouted. "Oh, my God, let me
get a shot of it. I'll go to church next Sunday, I swear. Oh,
Jupiter and Mithra, just one shot, that's all I ask!" Suddenly
the lizard leaped onto Dillis's head, threshed through his
tangled hair, and escaped down his back. He screamed, "I
missed it, I missed it!"

As they hiked on, Connie asked Humphrey, "Is he always like this?"

"Yes, or worse. He suffers from diarrhea of the mouth.
He can't keep still no matter what."

"He was probably hyperactive as a kid," she said. "Sometimes they never get over it. You have to admit he's kind of
funny. At least you know he's alive."

Near evening they came to a spot where the canyon,
joined by a ravine, widened. "This is the place I had in
mind to camp," said Connie. During spring rains, water
plunged from a channel a hundred feet overhead. Now all
was dry except for a shimmering brown pool at the base of
the plunge. On the surrounding cliffs ancient Indians had
pecked petroglyphs: spirals, zigzags, circles, snakes, bears,
and human legs and torsos topped by weird insect heads.

"Excellent!" said Dillis. "These will serve immoderately
well. Oh, I feel fine, I feel brimming! Thank you, Harriet,
for forcing me to bring along my paints." He strode back
and forth on the slickrock before the pool, brow furrowed,
an arm behind his back, cleated boots clattering. "Isn't this
a remarkable gallery? Look at it — vertical walls lightly decorated by petroglyphs, scantily hung, you might say, with
minor primitive works; space to let, room for the work of a
mighty modern, who has now arrived in my person."

Connie turned to Humphrey and Harriet. "The more I
think about all this the less I like it. I really don't think we
should let him mess up that cliff."

"Mess up? Improve, rather!" Dillis protested. "Dear girl, don't be alarmed. Here in this remote gorge we are pleased to observe the beginning of a scholarly tradition, the birth of a great controversy in the archeology of the southwestern United States. In the minds of many, this painting of an animal extinct for some 12,000 years will become evidence for the presence of homo sapiens in ice age Utah. Others will declare it a forgery, a deliberate fraud. Think of the scores of graduate students who will weigh the proofs on either side. Think of the scholarly literature that will accumulate. Think of the fillip this debate will add to the banquettings, inebriations, and sightseeings of many an academic conference."

"Mister, you flipped your lid a long time ago," Connie said.

"You're not to take all he says at face value," Harriet cautioned. "Dillis is a very metaphorical person."

"If he comes down on a rope, I'm of half a mind to go to the top and cut it."

"Ye gods! I believe she would!" Dillis said. "My heart goes out to you, Humphrey, domiciled as you are with a fire-breathing virago."

"Please, everyone, let's not cross streams till we come to them," Harriet said. "Let's make camp and build a nice fire and have a comfortable night's rest and see how things sort out in the morning."

The campers unlaced their packs, set up tents, and unrolled sleeping bags. Then, while the others watched, Dillis solemnly peeled off his clothes and folded them neatly on a rock. "Anyone for a swim?" he asked, entirely nude. When no one replied, he mumbled, "Apparently not." He picked his bare-footed way to the pool and waded in. After a few cautious strokes he began to bellow an aria. "Most invigorating," he shouted to the others. "Come in, come in!" Humphrey swung his back to the spectacle, shook out aspirins, and downed them with gulps from his canteen.

For nearly a quarter hour Dillis dove, swam, and floated,

all the while shouting and singing at full voice. He emerged from the pool, squatted on a mudbar, took up a handful of mud, and smeared his chest. With sudden energy he threw his body into the bar, rolling and writhing till he was covered with mud. He butted his head into the bar, bellowing like a bull, matting his hair. "I'm a water buffalo, a bison, an aurochs," he shouted. Compulsively Humphrey turned and, like the others, stared in open-mouthed amazement.

Dillis flung handfulls of mud against a boulder. "Instantaneous art," he explained loudly; "man creating, the artist seen in the quintessential nanosecond of the creative act." He squatted on a rock and defecated. He hoisted the feces onto his palm and painted it onto a boulder with two fingers. He hummed and mumbled, "This in the name of Raphael. And that for thee and none other, venerable Rembrandt."

"For Christ's sake, Dillis," Harriet commanded, "wash yourself and put on your pants."

"Unshackle yourself, woman!" Dillis exploded. "Reject the tyranny of the diaper. Storm the Bastille of your toilet training. Anal retentives of the world, arise. Leave your mark on every clean linoleum. Make an unsanitary deposit in every kitchen sink."

"No more of this sideshow for me," Humphrey said. "I've had enough. I'm going back to the ranch." He crawled into his tent on hands and knees and began to reroll his sleeping bag.

"I thought I performed rather brilliantly," called Dillis, who was washing himself in the pool. "But it appears I've overdone it again."

"You don't know the meaning of moderation," said Harriet. She followed Humphrey to his tent and knelt beside his protruding hindquarters. "Please don't abandon us no matter how offended you are," she said to Humphrey. "Give us a little time to mull our next step. Look, Dillis is dressed now. What would it take to persuade you to stay? I'm utterly distressed. I was so sure we could rub along with something close to tolerance for one another."

Humphrey backed from the tent. Still kneeling, he looked to his wife with beseeching eyes.

"He wants to drop out," Connie said to Harriet. "He wants to quit his Ph.D. program. He says it hurts too bad when he sees professors who act like Dillis. I can't say I blame him. Everywhere Dillis lights, maggots show up. Humphrey doesn't respect you anymore either. He says you're not up to much if you don't have better sense than to get involved with Dillis. He thinks you're worse than a kidnapper or an embezzler for telling Dillis it's okay to paint a forgery on a cliff."

Harriet swayed unsteadily for a moment. She seated herself on a nearby boulder and brushed an ear three or four times as if dislodging an insect. "What a devastating thought!" she said. "Have you really considered dropping out of your Ph.D. program? Have I been so cruel a taskmaster? Have I been so dictatorial and unapproachable?"

Dillis stepped forward. "Stop debasing yourself, Harriet! This is incredible! If he wants to drop out of grad school, let him. In fact, you should insist upon it. I've doubted his competence all along. Flunk him out and be thankful you've uncovered his bogus nature in time."

"You stay out of this," she said angrily. "Not another word!"

"That's right! Put down the only one who gives a damn about you. Not another word? So be it. Neither now nor later." He walked stiffly away.

Humphrey wrung his hands. "This is a dreadful confrontation. Pieces are starting to fly in all directions. Perhaps we should all beg one another's pardon and get on as best we can."

"No, you must tell me everything. Obviously I've deceived myself shamefully. I thought we were a teacher and a student who had cleared away the petty formalities. It seemed we were such good friends."

"He doesn't want to know about your love life," Connie said.

"No, and I don't want to know about the history of feminine hygiene."

"My goodness, you're very delicate, aren't you? I had no idea."

"We think it's mean of you to cheat on poor Preston," Connie said.

"Yes," agreed Humphrey, "we have felt very bad for Preston."

"Well, of course you would, wouldn't you? What can I say? It would have been more honest to divorce him. I thought I had chosen the kinder way. But tell me everything."

"That's all," Humphrey said. "I just want to quit."

"Well, you can't quit. I won't hear of it. I confess I'm terribly embarrassed. I see clearly how you could feel imposed upon. I've made you privy to my appalling confusions. I promise to do better. I'll keep my private life to myself. Will that be all right? Will you give up this idea of dropping out?"

He threw another helpless glance toward Connie, who shrugged her shoulders and said, "It's four years down the drain if you quit."

"There's another little problem close at hand here," he said. "I'm sorry to be so squeamish but I wish we could camp somewhere else."

"This is a nice spot," Connie said.

"I couldn't camp here. That boulder Dillis smeared turns my stomach."

Connie squinted into the pale arch of the sky. "It's nearly dark. There isn't another good camping place for miles."

Harriet stood and looked about. Dillis sat on a low ledge beyond the pool, tapping on a hand-held rock with a climber's pick. His dangling heels bounced against the ledge in time with his tapping.

"Please, Dillis," Harriet called, "we've got to spend the night with some show of civility toward one another. Won't you prove your contrition by cleaning the rock you've dirtied?"

He paused while she spoke. "You gotta be kidding," he said and resumed his tapping.

"He won't clean it off in a hundred years," Connie said. She turned to Humphrey. "You can put up with it. You don't have to be that fussy. Let's get on with our chores while there's light to see. Go up the ravine and get us some firewood while we start supper."

Humphrey climbed the ravine and foraged for wood among the junipers above the canyon rim. He tossed dead trunks into the canyon and the walls echoed the brittle crash. He watched from the rim while Connie dragged some of the wood to the camp and started a fire. He was thinking it was he, not Connie, who was the ignoramus; it was he, not Connie, who lacked an essential knowledge.

When he returned to camp, the women were preparing a stew. He sat cheerlessly before the fire and listened to Harriet, who was telling Connie that Cirencester, then called Corinium, had been second only to London among the towns of Roman Britain. Connie cast what seemed to be considerate glances toward her. Compared to the blond, buxom Connie, Harriet was willowy and slight. A blue bandanna covered her hair; Vibram-soled boots encased her feet. There was in Harriet's voice, he fancied, a subdued and palsied tone. As for himself, he doubted he would sleep at all during the coming night.

"If you could watch the stew," Harriet said to Connie, "I have another task to perform."

Stepping carefully in the twilight, she gathered dried, long-stemmed grass and bound it into a simple brush. "There's a pleasure in constructing a tool from whatever materials are at hand," she said. "Now to test the utility of my creation."

Humphrey's eyes, dazzled by the bright fire, followed her dark form. She scooped water from the pool with a pail and splashed it on the boulder Dillis had smeared. Bending, she scrubbed the rock with her makeshift brush. It appeared that Dillis, who still sat on the ledge, was watching; at least he made no motion or sound. Harriet finished scrubbing and splashed more water. She washed her hands and returned to the fire.

"That was a horrible thing to have to do," Humphrey said.

She replied, "I simply want a pleasant camp."

Connie set out four bowls and filled them with stew. Those at the fire took up their bowls and ate. "You'd better come," Harriet called to Dillis. "Your stew is cooling fast." He remained motionless on the ledge, scarcely visible in the flickering yellow light.

Harriet set down her bowl and went to him. When she stood before him, she had become no more than a vague, thin form in the darkness. "Won't you come to dinner?" she said.

"I had no inkling you would make yourself the charwoman of my latrine," he lamented.

"It's done and finished. Let's just go forward from this point. Maybe this can be a pleasant outing after all."

"You've anointed my feet with spikenard, you've wiped them with your tresses. You're the tenderest, the whitest, the most virginal of flowers."

"Please don't say such things. Especially please don't say them here."

Their voices had come to Humphrey in cadences oddly muted by the surrounding cliffs. He heard a scuffle of feet which he took to be Dillis jumping from the ledge. He heard a cough, a gasp, a sob. "Oh, Jesus, I love you," the weeping Dillis said.

She led him to the fire where they sat cross-legged opposite Humphrey and Connie. She placed his bowl in his hands and took up her own. Fixing his eyes upon his bowl, he spooned stew into his mouth. His cheeks glistened in the firelight. She watched a moment, then spoke to the young couple. "He's not a bad person. He's terribly complex. He's afflicted by impulses you can scarcely comprehend. He knows beauty's intimate texture but believes himself incapable of creating it. He's inconsolable to have discovered that his talent isn't grand but merely competent. Can you condemn him for that?"

Humphrey stared intently into the fire. He saw the red-cheeked face of Mr. Huggin, Trullydon's farmer. He saw the sparrow in Miss Throckmorton's ivy. He saw Professor Turmainder, drunk and stripped to his shorts and under-shirt. He saw the cliffs and catchpool, the slickrock, sagebrush, and willows, which stood just now beyond the perimeter of firelight. There was a reason, he was thinking, why so-called civilized persons should enter wilderness, to learn from its sheer otherness that they were both animal and angel.

On the following Monday Humphrey returned to his office and continued his dissertation. Every morning there-after Harriet passed his open door with a pleasant good morning but didn't come in. In time he submitted a chapter which she returned with polite suggestions for revision. These he attempted to heed as if they were the sternest, most ex-plicit of instructions. Almost hourly he vacillated between dreading a change in her mood and vilifying himself for the great embarrassment he had caused her.

On a Saturday evening in September, he and Connie took the girls to the state fair. They bought hot dogs and wandered about the blazing midway, where a ferris wheel circled, a calliope shrilled, and hawkers shouted. After they had given their daughters a ride on a merry-go-round, they abandoned the midway for the exhibition halls. They went first to the goats, on whose amiable personalities they de-pended for the entertainment of their children. A nanny with drooping ears and a bulging, two-teated udder nib-bled at Lena's finger; a half-grown kid, its forelegs propped upon a railing, accepted Helen's cautious caress. By the time they emerged from the goat building, Helen had conve-niently gone to sleep in her stroller. However, Lena, whom

Humphrey alternately carried and led by the hand, became increasingly querulous as they proceeded through the buildings where hogs and beef cattle were displayed.

"I think we'd better give it up and go home," Humphrey said.

"Not till we've visited the sewing crafts," Connie said. "I won't feel like I've even been to the fair if I don't look at the quilts."

Connie pushed the sleeping Helen vigorously forward. Humphrey hefted Lena onto a shoulder and followed, remembering from other years his wife's languorous inspections of dresses, doilies, sweaters, and quilts. Within moments, passing a pavilion where a country band played raucous music, they came face to face with Harriet and Dillis.

"Humphrey! Connie!" Dillis cried. "What a lucky encounter! Fate has sent you to salvage our evening. Have you ever seen so many disagreeable people gathered into one place in all your life? Every slovenly, unkempt redneck in Utah has shown up with his girlfriend and her kids! How I hate the impoverished classes. Why don't they keep themselves out of sight?"

"There but for the grace of God go we," Harriet reprimanded. Having greeted Humphrey and Connie, she disengaged her hand from Dillis's arm with what Humphrey supposed was the slightest display of shame. She wore a simple blue dress, casual shoes, no stockings. Her face, half shadowed by an overhead lamp, seemed limned by a chastened repose. The same overhead lamp cast moon shadows upon Dillis's deep seamed cheeks. He had, Humphrey was forced to admit, a dour, defiant handsomeness.

"Hullo, look who's here," said Dillis, bending down to examine the sleeping Helen. "Ah, now we look on beauty's own essential self, an innocent waif gone into the blissful arms of Morpheus."

He straightened, glared at a passing couple, and grimaced sourly. "I'm treading the slough of despond, my friends. Harriet and I have walked the terraces of hell with Dante and Virgil this evening. I am not referring to this despicable country band we've just escaped from, though that's certainly hellish enough. I mean we went through the fine arts exhibit a half hour ago. Why did God afflict the ungifted with the impulse to paint and sculpt? Unless I had seen it, I wouldn't have thought it humanly possible to gather so much ineptitude, so much gaucherie, under one roof."

"I told you you shouldn't go in there," said Harriet. "You really are masochistic."

Lena, who had so far nestled quietly in her father's arms, now twisted and whined, "I wanna go home!" Her blond hair, parted, pulled tight, and braided, glistened beneath the lamp.

"Lena, my girl," Dillis exclaimed, "you haven't so much as said hello. Don't you remember Dillis who went with you to your grandaddy's ranch? I'm the one who bought you root beer when we stopped for gas. I'm the one who entertained you with stories about goblins and fairies."

"I remember," she said.

"She does!" he shouted. "You wonderful child! Can I hug you? Will you come here to me for a minute?"

He stretched out his arms. She looked into her father's eyes. Humphrey squeezed her, then handed her to Dillis.

"What shall I buy you tonight? What in all this fantastical paradise of red-necked Mormons can Dillis buy for his little princess? An ice cream bar, for sure, and then let's go to those booths on the other side of the midway where they sell trinkets and toys and lacy little dresses. Would you like a necklace or a bracelet or maybe a little stuffed dog?"

"A necklace," she said.

"By all means, a necklace!" he said. With an imperious hand, he waved the others forward. Holding Lena and talking volubly, he fell in beside Connie, who began to push the stroller.

"Indecisiveness certainly isn't one of his failings," Harriet said to Humphrey as they strolled behind. "If you let him, he'll carry you away like a spring torrent."

"Lena likes him," Humphrey replied. "Maybe she sees things in him I don't."

"He's not entirely unlikable, is he? He intends to be humorous, he wants to entertain. His problem is he goes over everybody's head. He's too oblique and allusive. He's certainly trying to make amends to you and Connie. I'm sure he thinks he's making a display of contrition. He feels very bad about our trip into the canyon. He thinks he behaved very unkindly. He admires you and Connie, and in his own backward way he loves your little girls."

"I'm getting used to him," Humphrey said.

Dillis and Connie, by now some distance ahead, were leading them through the building where rabbits were on exhibit. A pungent odor hung in the cavernous hall. In hundreds of small wire cages rabbits of innumerable sizes and colors fed, hopped, or lolled.

Harriet paused beside a cage and pointed. Inside were a mother rabbit and a half grown litter of a spotted variety. The young rabbits, intent upon suckling, pursued the female relentlessly; she, equally determined to escape her brood, bounced desperately back and forth within the tiny cage. By moments she halted, panting and quivering, whereupon her offspring wriggled beneath her with aggressive vigor. An instant later, the harried female leapt into another series of frenzied bounces, her young again scrambling and colliding like miniature football players.

"My God," Harriet said, "they'll run her to death. They're intent on their own welfare, not hers. It's a rape, a murder. I never saw more clearly in all my life how offspring prey upon their parents."

"Maybe it's the crowd. Maybe when everybody's gone and the lights are out, she'll settle down and let them nurse."

"They're big enough to eat pellets. Why don't they?"

Humphrey peered into the cage. "They're out of pellets," he said. "Hopefully someone will be along pretty soon with their evening ration."

"It's uncanny how trivial encounters magnify our

perplexities," Harriet said as the mother rabbit launched into another desperate dash. "My husband was so eager to make love the night I flew in from England. Can you imagine what a woman has to do to help a man in Preston's condition make love? Thank God the frenzy doesn't visit him often. And Dillis isn't much of an improvement. When we first fell in love, he was so attentive, so solicitous and tender. Now he's dark and moody and has to be cajoled and petted."

She stooped, picked up hay from beneath another cage, and, stem by stem, pushed it into the cage of the fleeing mother rabbit. Immediately the little rabbits began to eat and the panting mother withdrew to an opposite corner. "There, I've done my good turn for the day," Harriet said. "But I promised you I wouldn't speak of intimate things ever again. Please forgive me."

She went forward briskly, Humphrey following. They went outside in time to watch Dillis and Connie enter the dairy cattle hall. "It's rather strange to see them together," Harriet said. "They seem to be getting on well. Your Connie is an admirable person. She has her feet planted very solidly."

"Yes, I was lucky to marry her. I depend on her a great deal."

"I'm glad we've met this evening on what we might call neutral ground. I've wanted to justify certain things to you ever since our trip into the canyon. I think I should tell you Dillis has painted his rhinoceros on a cliff in a canyon he and I backpacked into a couple of weeks ago. The truth is I've gone back to Dillis completely."

"Yes, I thought it likely you would."

They entered the cattle hall and paused to watch an attendant give water to a large-boned Holstein. At length the cow, water dribbling from her muzzle, looked around at Humphrey and Harriet.

"Did you ever hear me lecture on Sir Francis Bacon's habit of drinking the water in which he had washed his face each morning?" Harriet asked.

"No, I never heard you speak of that."

"History is full of incredible facts," she said. "Another is the pierced cheek of Peter Throckmorton, the Trumpet of Cirencester. Because of that unhealed cheek, they say, his sermons were accompanied by a kind of whistling echo."

"I would like to put that in my dissertation."

"But of course you can't. You have to keep faith with Priscilla Throckmorton, who has treated us very generously."

"That's true," he said.

The attendant now led the cow from the stall and positioned her on a milking ramp. He washed her giant udder and fixed suction cups to her teats. The milking machine began to pump with soft rhythmical surges.

"I don't suppose I can persuade you," Harriet went on, "that it is the most orderly, the most faithful thing I could possibly do to cherish Dillis with my former fervor. I confess to have entertained the girlish fancy that all that lacked to rocket me into a high, rare atmosphere was a proper ignition. But now I think it is quite natural, quite inevitable, that passion must subside into duty."

"I don't think you need to persuade me," he said. "It isn't any of my business."

"Of course not. And here I am filling your ear with personal matters again."

"I don't mind."

"I think maybe you really don't," she said. "But I'll try not to mention them again."

She walked on toward Dillis and Connie who waited in the far door. Humphrey lingered to watch the milker for a moment. He found himself mourning that he had ignorantly precluded himself from Harriet's confidences. From one perspective he had judged them to be an affront; now, from another, they seemed an honor. Then he cheered up and followed her, willing to believe again, as he had in former times, that there had been no canker in the root of the Renaissance.

THE GOATS OF TIMPANOGOS

FOR FORTY YEARS CLIFFORD WORSHIPPED HIS WIFE,
an affectionate, beautiful woman named Dixie. He also worshipped tobacco. From his teen years he had savored the
aroma of the crumbled leaf, relished the taste of smoke,
delighted in the percolation of nicotine through his lungs.
Of course he didn't smoke in the presence of his wife and
children. He was a thoughtful companion, a kind father,
and, by virtue of his success as a grocer, an ample provider.
He was even a willing tithe payer and regular attender at
church despite the natural reluctance of a backslider to sit
among the worthy. Every Sunday during church he allowed
the consecrated bread and water to go by untasted. When it
had been time to name, baptize, or confirm each of his five
children, he had ceded a father's right to perform these
ceremonies to a brother or a friend. By simple inertia he
defied Dixie's dearest wish, which was that their marriage
be sealed for eternity in the temple, for, though a smoker
might be tolerated in the meetinghouse on Sunday, he was
forbidden to enter the holy temple.

On summer evenings when their children were small,
they often went to the lake for a picnic. Following their
meal Clifford strolled in solitude along the shore while he
smoked an evening cigarette. Sometimes he could have wept
from shame because his children knew only too well why

they were forbidden to accompany him. On other occasions, while he watched the lake and mountains and pastel sky gather into darkness, he experienced an inexplicable happiness. The lake seemed wild and sacred, and he felt himself to be at one with its reedy odors, its silvered expanse, its solemn splash. In those moments he was reconciled to his destiny as an unvaliant son of God. It no longer seemed to matter that in eternity he would be separated from his devoted wife, his wonderfully innocent children, his excellent parents, his faithful brothers and sisters.

Shortly before Clifford turned sixty, Dixie died of a stroke. Despite the proximity of two of his married daughters, who invited him to dinner with thoughtful frequency, Clifford suffered an excruciating loneliness. Each evening he returned with dread to the emptiness of his house on the east bench of Provo. Late one night he awoke from a passionate dream in which his wife had been young and startlingly wanton. The dream had seemed so real that it intensified his loneliness. It also filled him with shame, for Dixie had regarded erotic dreams as a kind of promiscuity.

The next morning Clifford confided his morbid state of mind to Seraphine, the manager of his convenience store in Payson and a woman of enormous bones and obese flesh. "I think I'm having a nervous breakdown," he said. "I can't get over thinking about how Dixie looked in her coffin."

"Now that's just silly," she protested. "You're not having any nervous breakdown."

"I dreamed about Dixie last night. Sometimes it seems she is still in the house. I mean her spirit, of course."

"Well, maybe she is still there in the house. She wants to comfort you, you poor lonely boy," Seraphine said.

"She was a beautiful woman," he said. "Her nose and cheeks and chin were very delicate. Everybody always said so. She kept herself very trim while I went to seed, losing my hair and sagging in the belly. People always wondered why she married me. She was very spiritual. I was nothing but a drag on her. I'm not sure she'd want to be sealed to me for eternity."

"Of course she wants to be sealed to you for eternity," Seraphine remonstrated. "Now you just get a grip on yourself and stop thinking dismal thoughts. You'll feel a thousand times better when you've quit smoking and gone to the temple and got this sealing business finished and over with."

At mid-morning, Clifford visited Dixie's grave. Filthy snow mantled the cemetery and a ceiling of dense clouds stifled the sky. Failing to find comfort, he drove to the lake. The grey, desolate water, threshed by a rising wind, only increased his anxiety. Mist swirled, snow pelted his face, and the waves heaved great blocks of ice against the shore with shock and violence. Never before had he perceived how lethal and uncaring, how unregenerate and chaotic, wilderness was. He retreated to his automobile, weeping over his vulnerability and berating his wife for having abandoned him. He returned along the icy rural lane amidst a blizzard, his windshield wipers scraping a bleary patch of visibility. He prayed as he drove, promising God that he would purify and perfect himself and become the disciplined, self-denying person Dixie had always wished him to be. With special fervor he pleaded for an apparition of his wife. If he could have even so little as a fleeting glimpse of her, he would content himself; he would limp across his remaining years in uncomplaining silence.

He took a late lunch at the snack bar of his Orem store. When he had finished, he lit a cigarette and stared moodily through the plate glass window. In a moment a woman with a tray in her hands asked whether she could join him. She apologized for her forwardness, saying that early in the morning she had had a premonition that she was to have lunch at this particular table. "Do you believe in premonitions?" she asked.

"I suppose it depends on which kind of premonition you mean," he said. "Sometimes God tells people things in advance. However, he never has told me anything in advance. Of course I haven't deserved to know anything in advance."

They regarded the diminishing storm outside. "I never worry about storms," she said brightly. "A snowstorm is an energy flume, a tremendous restorative."

"I don't want you to get the wrong impression of me," he said, tapping his cigarette on an ash tray. "I'm smoking my last pack. I'm going to quit cold turkey in the morning." He had no idea why he felt obliged to assure her that he often went to church and made it the major concern of his life to earn an honest living.

She said her name was Sheila and she was supervisor of a ladies fashions floor in the nearby mall. She said she too was a church-goer and seemed impressed to learn that he owned this store. Shortly the clouds parted and they caught sight of sunlight gleaming upon the virgin snow of Timpanogos. "There are wild goats in the high north canyons of Timpanogos at this very instant," she said. "It's unbelievable that they can survive the winter there."

She was thin and ill-postured; her teeth were too prominent, her nose beaked, her raven hair undoubtedly dyed. Nonetheless, there was an anomalous vitality about her, a cheerful glow in which a chilled bystander might warm his hands. She seemed heroically capacious with sympathy and fellow feeling, and without forethought Clifford found himself divulging the sorrow of his wife's death.

"I didn't mean to let her slip away without giving her that big surprise she was waiting for. Every few months I'd think it was getting time to tell her I was ready to go to the temple. But of course I kept putting it off. She was a tremendous woman. Very spiritual. She was the kind of woman a man shouldn't use in a carnal way. I knew that, but I couldn't help myself. I was like every other husband. I took advantage of her good nature. And now I'm suffering terribly. I need to know how I stand with her. Maybe she doesn't want me for eternity. Maybe it's too late. I wouldn't blame her at all if she's given up on me."

"Of course she hasn't given up on you," Sheila said. "It's marvelous how my premonitions are always right. I had a feeling this morning before I got out of bed that this would be an unusual day. This just shows you, storms bring convergences. The instant I saw you sitting here at this booth I knew who you were. I know Dixie. She's a silver-haired woman with beautiful brows and cheeks. As you say, she's very spiritual. I saw her yesterday while I was reviewing invoices in my office. I admit it's unnerving to see the dead, but I've learned to control my feelings. In their own good time, the dead will let you know what they want. I knew this beautiful silver-haired woman couldn't rest. I knew there was something unsettled in the life she had just left. It's very clear now, isn't it? There's no question what she wants. She wants you to go to the temple and be sealed to her as soon as you can. I'm sure of that."

Head bent, eyes averted, Clifford wept. "I'm sorry for you," Sheila said. "I hope you'll find comfort soon. It's true grief is very foolish. All those sad things we think we see are reflections in a distorted mirror. In the great cosmic center everything is serene. But who has the self-discipline to remember that fact when troubles come? Who can help feeling bad?"

She began to recite her own grief. Her husband had taken her to a resort for a tennis vacation, hoping to soften the blow of his sudden announcement that he wanted a divorce. The night of his announcement they had lain in bed, he reading a novel, she nestling against him, soaking his shoulder with tears. "But I have learned that my divorce was for the best," she said. "I want to purify myself just as you do. It is very hard to purify yourself if you are married. It is also hard if you are a parent. June and Jimmy are such fine children. It won't be long and they'll graduate from high school and then I suppose they'll want to move away, won't they? I admit that will be very hard for me. I admit I will be very, very lonely. But at least I will be able to live on my own terms. You have a duty to your children, you know, an obligation to show them the world and let them make their own choices about it."

She stood and gathered soiled napkins and cups onto her tray. "Would you like to go to church with June and Jimmy and me?" she asked. Instantly she seemed embarrassed. "Goodby. I hope I've helped you a little. I hope you'll feel better soon."

The next morning, while he cooked and ate his oatmeal, Clifford apologized to Dixie for feeling so attracted to the uncanny woman he had met in his Orem store. He said to the empty sink, where he imagined Dixie stood, "You had a chance, you know. You could have appeared to me instead of to her. But if that's the way you want to do it, I'll just have to put up with it."

After eating he lit a cigarette. The possibility that Dixie stood nearby yet refused to appear seemed very cruel. "I really am going to quit smoking," he said on the chance that she listened. "As for Sheila, either she's very spiritual or she's crazy. She believes in energy vortexes and she loves the wild goats on Timpanogos. I promise I'll watch myself closely. I won't let myself get attached to her. Not that she'd be interested in a man of my age anyhow. But, jeez, Dixie, I hope you'll do your part! Please let me know you're okay and do it pretty soon. I can't take much more of this loneliness."

On Sunday he accompanied Sheila and her children to church. The children proved to be pleasant, though not handsome, June having acne and straight yellow hair and Jimmy having, like his mother, a beaked nose planted upon a long, hollow face. During the service they sat on either side of Clifford, as if the rules of hospitality required it. Sheila, seated on the other side of Jimmy, wore a flowered silk dress which clung to her willowy thighs. Clifford was impressed by how intently she listened to the sermon. The preacher spoke against taking sin lightly, claiming that a serious sin like embezzlement or adultery required a profound agony on the part of the penitent and a proper confession to the authorities of the church.

At supper in Sheila's apartment following the service,

they discussed the sermon. "Why can't you repent directly to God?" June asked. "Why should you have to confess to a man?"

"She's worried about her sins," Jimmy said. "She's been up to all kinds of bad things."

"Oh, barf," June said. "Our seminary teacher says it's simple. You just have to make up your mind. I've decided I'm never going to commit any sins. I mean big sins, the kind you'd have to confess. I couldn't stand to do it."

Sheila served Clifford a tomato stuffed with tiny shrimp and celery bits. He sliced it carefully and took delicate bites. "I imagine," Sheila said, "there could be a kind of stark pleasure in confessing a terrible sin. It would be such a triumph over the appetite for respectability. We're all controlled by public opinion. We'd rather be respectable than eat or sleep."

With a guilty start Clifford awakened to the fact that for an hour he had not thought about Dixie; for an hour he had been very happy. For the first time he noticed that Sheila had misaligned eyes. It seemed possible that when she was looking at him she was also looking at something else. What she had said about a triumph over appetite made great sense to him. It cheered him enormously to recognize how ardently he yearned for self denial.

Following the meal Clifford helped Sheila with the dishes. Her apartment was a basement in a shabby quarter of Provo. On a tiny lacquered table in a corner sat an elegant porcelain tea set. On her bed, visible through an open door, were ruffled pillows and a flowered spread. As Clifford dried dishes, his elbow brushed hers. She glanced, caught his eye, smiled. She faced him and put her arms around his neck, dangling her dripping hands behind him. She offered her cheek and he kissed it.

"Do you think I'm supposed to help you?" she murmured.

"I don't know."

"At any rate I mustn't be a hindrance to you, must I? I

think I will never go to the temple. But that doesn't mean
that you shouldn't. I don't sleep well lately. I am rather
obsessed by Dixie. You haven't stopped smoking, have you?
Shouldn't you do it at once? There is nothing less selfish, no
greater triumph over flesh and matter, than to be loyal to a
dead loved one."

Again she offered her cheek and he kissed it. "I have a
crystal for you, a very potent one," she said. "It's small
enough to carry in your wallet. If it radiates too much power,
you can carry it in your coat pocket instead of your wallet.
It will help you stop smoking." She hugged him again and
murmured as she released him, "I promise I'll be a help
and not a hindrance."

The next morning while he ate breakfast, he addressed
his empty kitchen sink. For a moment it seemed Dixie truly
stood there listening. "It'll be all right, honey. Sheila has a
lot of loose springs inside her head, but there's no question
she's looking out for you and me. I'm thinking of her exactly
like a sister, exactly like I think of Seraphine, and, good
hell, Seraphine hugs me all the time and you don't worry
about that, do you? I promise I won't get attached to Sheila.
Look here, I haven't had a cigarette since yesterday morning. I've quit, I really have!"

A little later at his Payson store he told Seraphine he
had attended church with a divorced woman and her children. "What do you think?" he asked. "Is it wrong to get
tangled up in a friendship with a woman when you know
you're never going to marry her?"

"Lordy, you poor sorrowing boy!" his store manager said,
squeezing his hand in an iron grip. "You don't have to apologize to me about getting married again. Maybe not just
yet, of course, but when you've waited a decent bit of time,
I do absolutely hope you'll ask somebody to marry you. I
certainly do."

However, when he named Sheila, Seraphine became belligerent. "Well, now, that's a horse of a different color! You
might have told me who she was to start with instead of

leading me to think you'd met some nice widow over at the singles ward. I'll just talk straight with you, even if you are my employer. I happen to know a good deal about Sheila. It so happens this nice lady you went to church with holds seances and sees through walls and looks into the other world through big magnetic funnels. For once in your life you just listen to me. You drop that lady like a hot potato."

During the weeks which followed, Seraphine asked suspicious questions of Clifford, which he answered evasively. The truth was that by the time spring came, he had made a comfortable habit of Sheila. He went shopping with her, took her for drives, and came often at night to her apartment for supper, always bringing along a large sack of groceries. He had to admit that, despite all her attempts to appear as a sound, regular church member, Sheila often slipped into allusions to the occult. Even worse, she was unconsciously sensuous, allowing her body to flex in a provocative way when she laughed, and he often suffered from erotic dreams about her. Yet thanks to the crystal she had given him, which on certain astonishing occasions seemed to buzz like a hive of bees, he succeeded in giving up smoking and arranged with his bishop for his first visit to the temple.

Clifford made plans to go to the temple with Gaylene and Ellie, his daughters who lived in Utah County. It was agreed he would participate only in the ceremony of the endowment, waiting to be sealed to Dixie in eternal marriage on her birthday when their other children also promised to be present. Not long before the appointed day, his daughters called on him at the small warehouse attached to his Center Street store. They had been to an art exhibit in Springville and wore high heels and elegant dresses. Gaylene was short, stout, and energetic; she had never been tolerant of Clifford's weaknesses. Ellie was thin and perpetually worried. Neither was as beautiful as her mother.

Clifford brought chairs from the office and went on loading a van with canned goods destined for his other stores.

"You need a vacation," Gaylene said. "You've turned into a can of peas."

"I golf once a week when the weather's good," Clifford said.

"What a dusty place this is. I haven't been here for years. You ought to become an art dealer. You could hang paintings on all these big bare walls. Thank goodness the girlie calendars are gone."

"I didn't know you kids ever came into this warehouse. You weren't supposed to."

"Oh, we came here all the time," said Ellie. "Those calendars were depressing. I knew a skinny, flat-chested thing like me didn't have any chances at all."

Gaylene asked whether he had bought his temple clothes. He said he had: pants, shirt, tie, socks, robe, and cap, all white as snow.

"Don't expect too much from the endowment ceremony," Gaylene said. "There's nothing so marvelous about it. Don't let yourself be disappointed."

"There's everything marvelous about it!" Ellie protested. "People see angels in the temple. They see their dead loved ones. They hear God's voice."

"Things like that don't happen very often," Gaylene said. "You know how people are. They tell all kinds of stories. It's just a ceremony. You put on your celestial robe and apron and make promises to endure to the end."

Clifford trundled his dolly down an aisle between towering boxes, his daughters following. Gaylene paused before a stack of boxed paper towels. "These are terribly inferior," she said. "They'll hardly absorb a teaspoon of liquid. Why don't you sell a better brand?"

"I sell what my customers seem willing to buy," he said.

Clifford was not surprised, he was in fact waiting, when Gaylene said, "Daddy, it doesn't mean we don't love you if we say things you maybe would rather not hear. We're proud of you for quitting smoking and getting ready to go to the temple. But I think we should have a talk with you about that woman you've been seeing. I had a call from Seraphine who manages your Payson store. It's awfully worrisome if what she says is true."

"Oh, don't bring that up now, Gaylene," Ellie pleaded. "Let's not ruin such a nice, relaxed day."

"You're such a fussbudget, Ellie," Gaylene said. "You don't have the nerve of a polliwog. It doesn't seem right for Daddy to be courting another woman when he is getting ready to go back to the temple on Mama's birthday and be sealed to her in eternal marriage. It's just like him to quit smoking and pretend to clean up his behavior, and all the while he's still doing something behind Mama's back."

"Poor Daddy has as much right to a little earthly happiness as you do," Ellie insisted. "I don't notice you moving home to take care of him."

"Her name is Sheila," Clifford said. "She goes to church and has a couple of really fine kids who attend seminary and don't use bad language. I admit she's misguided in her notions, believing in crystals and chakras and things of that nature. She gave me a crystal and I never had another cigarette. I quit cold turkey. Got the crystal in my wallet right now. Of course it isn't the crystal that made me quit smoking. It was Sheila. She just said, 'You've got to quit; do it now.' "

"Crystals are from the dark side of the world," Gaylene said. "You shouldn't be carrying one in your wallet."

"I suppose you're right. You always are."

"Will you get rid of it? Will you stop seeing her?"

They paused at the dim end of the aisle, he leaning on the dolly. He wet the tip of a finger with his tongue and rubbed a spot on Gaylene's patent leather purse. "One of the kids must've got egg on your purse," he said. "Funny. You don't see egg on a purse very often."

"I don't think it'd be egg," she said.

"I guess it wouldn't be. If you think I ought to get rid of this crystal, I'll do it. It does seem foolish to carry it around. I can see your point of view about Sheila. A man who's had forty wonderful years with a woman like Dixie doesn't want another wife, here or hereafter."

"Oh, Daddy, I'd be so relieved if you really would break up with her!" Gaylene said.

On the evening before he went to the temple, Clifford brought Sheila to his house. They heated a can of spaghetti and carried their plates onto the rear deck. She leaned against the railing and told a story.

"A man came into the lingerie department today. By his clothes I'd judge he was a rancher. He seemed drowned in embarrassment among the racks of bras and panties and sheer nighties. He could only point to a pair of peach colored string bikini panties and then make a precise circle with his arms to indicate the size of his beloved. I asked whether he wanted a bikini bra to match. He blurted, 'It takes a lot of strap to hold her up,' took his package and fled."

Clifford laughed as he supposed she had meant him to do.

"I am remiss in my profession," Sheila said. "I'm a broker in dainty adornments of the female body. I should sell cloaks and gowns that would dampen lust and passion rather than rouse and entice them."

"You can't change human nature," Clifford said.

"But in that portion of it pertaining to ourselves we must. Isn't that true?"

He sat with his feet cocked upon the railing. Before him spread Utah Valley with its lighted grids of city streets, a darkening patchwork of farms, and the great silvered lake. "They say the temple is the holiest place on earth," he said.

"Yes, everyone says it is."

"But you say you'll never go there. It isn't in your plans."

"That's correct. It isn't in my plans."

"You're not really a Christian."

"Oh, yes, I'm very much a Christian."

"Some people think you're from the dark side of the earth."

"I won't ask who," she said. "I already know too many

who think so."

"Do you think I'll see Dixie in the temple tomorrow?" he asked.

"It's possible. Very possible."

"Dixie and I," he said sadly, "never quarreled; we never spoke angry words. But there was a certain way I felt about things that she didn't like. She hated it in me. She wanted to rub it out, to kill it. Naturally I didn't let her. I kept up the fight, I never gave in. But now isn't it odd? She's dead and I've surrendered."

"Don't you want to surrender?" Sheila said. "Don't you want to side with the spirit against the flesh?"

"I'm getting cold feet," he said. "By this time tomorrow I won't be the same man. Something will happen to me in the temple. I'll come out with something missing, like a lung or a kidney. I think maybe I don't want to go."

"Of course you want to go. You must go. Something very extraordinary and fine will happen to you. And of course a part of your former self will then be missing. It will be as if your body has been flushed, every cell of it, by a sacred solvent. There will be less dross, less encumbrance."

His daughters picked him up at eight. Gaylene drove furiously, mashing the gas pedal after stop signs and braking abruptly in the temple parking lot.

"I don't know who's going to mother your kids when you get killed in a car accident," said Clifford, who sat in the rear.

"Getting here is what counts," Gaylene said, scowling into the mirror. "I hope you got rid of that crystal."

"I forgot to. It's still in my wallet." He extracted the tiny crystal and held it on his palm. It was the merest fragment of rock, coppery in hue and strangely curved like the beak of a minute eagle. When his daughters had seen it, he replaced it in his wallet.

"It's nothing but a rock," said Ellie.

"I don't think you ought to carry it into the temple," Gaylene said. "It doesn't seem right."

"I'll get rid of it right away."

"There's a garbage can right over there."

"I think I ought to return it to Sheila."

"I was hoping you wouldn't see her again." Gaylene gripped the steering wheel and stared steadily into his mirrored eyes.

"I couldn't just not see her again," he said. "That wouldn't be civilized. She has feelings like everybody else. But, good heavens, she's not a seductress. She knows things are coming to an end between us. She'll go away gently. That's her nature."

He pulled the small suitcase which held his temple clothes onto his lap and opened the door.

"I don't think you ought to carry that crystal into the temple," Gaylene repeated.

"Don't exaggerate its importance," Ellie said. "It's just a rock."

Clifford emerged from the men's washing and anointing room and joined his daughters in the chapel, where, amid soft, solemn music, they awaited the beginning of the endowment session. Others, similarly clad in white, took their seats with slight rustlings and occasional murmurs. He had no doubt of God's presence. Holiness was everywhere, permeating the air, replacing its oxygen, forcing his breath in suffocated pants. His long, wicked intransigence lay clearly before him. With fright he grasped why God preferred to manifest himself in a temple constructed by human hands, symbolic of that celestial realm where unruly matter had at last been transmuted into perfect obedience.

"You don't look good," said Ellie, clutching his hand.

"Do you think your mother is here?" he whispered.

In the pew ahead, a woman turned and held her finger to her lips, commanding silence.

Ellie crushed his fingers. "Oh, she's with us," she cried softly. "She's right here with us this very instant!"

Tears tracked upon Ellie's rapt, upturned face. "She forgives us for everything. Everything is all right now. Everything is healed. Everything is made whole."

"Please, God," he prayed silently, "let me see her. Let her tell me she still wants me."

Shortly the endowment ceremony began. It consisted in part of a simple movie, a projection upon a screen of an allegorical drama representing the passage of the human soul through the probation of this world and into the glory of the hereafter. At appropriate moments the congregation recited vows to maintain an exact obedience to God's commandments and donned their robes, aprons, and caps. Long before the ceremony ended, Clifford had lost hope, and by the time he returned to the men's dressing room, he had become so chilled and feverish that he wondered whether he was suffering an attack of flu.

Standing before a mirror tying a knot in his tie, he saw the root of his difficulty. The allegorical film, intended to reinforce his piety, had done the opposite. Upon the screen he had seen an actress playing the part of Mother Eve who had, like Sheila, a long face, an aquiline nose, and tumbling brunette hair. He had in fact been curiously enamored of the dark-haired Eve who succumbed to the blandishments of the Tempter, hid herself from the wrathful scrutiny of God, and submissively followed a crestfallen Adam out the gates of Eden into the fallen world. Though he had deplored such scandalous emotion in a holy place, Clifford had been unable to quell his lust for this beautiful mother of the human race.

Despite his best intentions, he saw as he finished knotting his tie, he had allowed himself to fall in love with Sheila, not with that fraternal affection which a Christian man should hold toward a godly woman but with a blatant passion. He entered a stall, lifted the toilet seat, and urinated. He could think of only a single recourse. With cautious fingers he removed the tiny crystal from his wallet. He flushed the toilet and dropped the crystal into the swirling liquid.

Outside Ellie and Gaylene took Clifford's either arm,

and the three strolled through the temple gardens in the bright May forenoon. Eastward loomed the Provo mountains, a magnificent blend of barren slopes, layered cliffs, and forested canyons. Northward stood Timpanogos in pale, abstract repose. Ellie chattered with animation, referring over and over to the miraculous apparition of her mother as a literal fact. Gaylene was silent and unsmiling.

"My daughters will pull me up from the quagmire of the world," said Clifford. "Ellie is merciful, and Gaylene is just. Justice and mercy, two wonderful medicines for an old, ailing man. I threw the crystal away. It's gone; it can't be found or brought back. I don't doubt it did me more harm than good. Thank you, Gaylene, for bringing me to my senses."

"I love you, Daddy," Gaylene said.

With that, father and daughters closed in a three-cornered embrace. Clasping his daughters amidst the flowers and shrubs and newly mown lawns of the temple grounds, Clifford believed himself strengthened for the austere and lonely years ahead.

That evening Sheila phoned him at home, and Clifford reported Dixie's apparition to Ellie as if he himself had witnessed it. Sheila professed herself to be thrilled. He didn't ask her out or offer to come by her apartment. A week later she phoned again and in a subdued voice asked whether he would donate his truck for transporting decorations for a reception and dance which would follow June's high school graduation. It was of course an innocent, urgent request he couldn't refuse, and he spent most of the following Thursday afternoon helping June and her friends saw and nail arches, railings, and lattices. Then, because June expected it, he accompanied Sheila to the graduation on the next evening.

During the reception which followed Clifford assisted at the refreshments table, ladling punch and recharging cookie trays. When the crowd of well-wishers had dissipated and the graduates had begun to dance, Sheila asked whether he would render a final small service. She had been invited to a garden party in Orem and would be grateful if he'd take her by. She promised they wouldn't stay long.

In the car she reapplied her dark lipstick. She wore a short dress; her exposed legs struck Clifford as extraordinarily provocative. At a stop light she said, "These past few days I have been very cruel with myself and very foolish. I was of half a mind to call you up and say, Clifford, please, if you've decided we're through, in the name of mercy tell me to my face so that I can stop wondering and waiting. But as I say, my feelings aren't so muddy now. It was very comforting to sit beside you during the graduation. It helped me sort things out properly. It's all right if you stop coming to see me. What else could we expect now that you've been to the temple and had a wonderful experience with Dixie?"

Though it was late and the buffet had been demolished hours before, the garden party continued unabated in this benign, balmy night. Sheila detached herself from Clifford and wandered from group to group, chatting affably. Clifford drifted to a railed overlook at the edge of the yard. Far away the temple floated golden white on a watery darkness. He heard the scrambling of feet and suddenly two women materialized from the night. They introduced themselves as Tammy and Cora, saying they had just achieved a foray to the river in the dark bottom below.

"We've heard a lot about you," Tammy said. "You must have heard about us too. We're Sheila's best friends. We're inseparable. We were Siamese triplets in a prior existence, joined at the left shoulder. At least we all have strange marks on our left shoulders."

They turned their eyes upon Sheila, who, seated upon a retaining wall, had begun to sing. It seemed very natural to Clifford to see appreciative friends clustered about her. Unquestionably she was a catalyst, a conveyor of energy and hope.

"She jogs with Tammy and me two or three times a

week," Cora said. "Poor Sheila. Her divorce has been hard on all of us. We like to do things as couples. Of course it was me who got divorced first. Now I'm married to Dan. Tammy told me Dan was the man for me a long time before I could see it myself. Tammy has wonderful insight into the male personality. Our husbands want to climb Timpanogos this summer. Maybe you'd come along so Sheila could join us. It'd be terrible to leave her behind. She wants to see the wild goats. She thinks she was a goat in a former life. I think that's stretching it a bit. But what does it hurt to believe something like that?"

Their husbands joined them. Dan was a distributor of petroleum products. Warren, Tammy's husband, was a range biologist at the university. Somebody had handed Sheila a guitar. She strummed it, found a pitch, and began to sing another love song. "Gotta get in on this," Tammy said, and she and Cora drifted away to the group clustered about their friends.

"So you're the prospective new husband," Warren said. "Welcome aboard. It'll be nice to get our little threesome going again."

"We've never said anything about getting married," Clifford said.

"Oops! Sorry about that." He gave Clifford an affectionate pat on the shoulder. "Well, I'm going to ramble over and listen to her sing. She's got an absolutely beautiful voice."

When Warren was out of hearing, Dan said, "It's not such an all-fired pretty voice. She cracks when she goes for a high note. Cora damn near worships Sheila; so does Tammy. They were roommates in college. I don't know how you would've predicted they were going to turn out as screwy as they have. Lucky for me, Cora's not as looped out as the other two. Sheila's worst of all, of course. She believes in reincarnation. She thinks she's been around for centuries and centuries trying to purify herself to the point where she can finally drown in the big cosmic lake and disappear for good. She's no more a believer in the church than that garden gate over there. She goes to church for her kids' sake. If the church authorities knew of some of the things she's into, seances and the like, they'd excommunicate her in ten seconds flat."

Driving Sheila home, Clifford steeled himself for saying goodby. When she asked him to come in, he agreed. They sat listlessly at the kitchen table. She asked him whether he would like a drink of milk. He said no. He wondered whether she would ask him to return her crystal. He decided to tell her he didn't know where he had lost it. He knew she expected him to make a clean and open break. He had no idea why it was so hard to begin. Absentmindedly she removed her lipstick with a tissue, which she deposited in a pail beneath the sink.

"That Jimmy!" she said. "I asked him to take out the garbage yesterday."

"I could take it out," Clifford offered.

"Certainly not. I'll get on his case in the morning."

Nonetheless, Clifford carried the overflowing pail to the garage behind the house. Finding no light switch, he returned to the apartment. Apologetically, he replaced the unemptied pail beneath the sink and sat again with Sheila.

"I think we'd be better off," he said, "if we didn't see each other any more."

"Yes, I believe so, too."

"Dan says you believe in reincarnation."

"I'm sure Dan would tell you about it in a negative way. He doesn't like me. The feeling is mutual. He's a sour, scornful man. I told Cora she shouldn't marry him."

"I'm not much on reincarnation myself," Clifford said.

"So I would expect. It isn't exactly popular around this vicinity."

"I don't see how you reconcile it with the church."

"I manage. The Bible's full of reincarnation. So's the Book of Mormon. If you really want to know about it, I'll show you."

"No, I guess I don't want to know," he said. "But if it

gives you pleasure, go ahead and believe in it."

"I don't have any choice. I have very clear memories from prior existences. I know I'm not mistaken."

"My gosh!"

"The first day I ever saw you in this body, that snowy day at your Orem store, I knew I had seen you before in another body. I knew I had once been your wife. That night at home I remembered. I think we lived on a farm. A war came, perhaps the Civil War, and you wouldn't be dissuaded. You volunteered and went away and you were killed. I lived to be an old, lonely woman. You can't guess how jealous I have been over Dixie. You can't imagine the self discipline it took to take her part. It was one of the most crucial tests I have ever undergone. And I didn't fail her, did I?"

"No, I guess you didn't."

"I'd better take that garbage out," she said.

Compulsively Clifford followed her to the garage. He stood in the dark interior listening while she clattered among the cans. The garage was redolent of molding orange rinds and putrefying meat scraps. As she returned to the door she bumped into him. She teetered on her high heels and dropped the pail. They caught one another's arms. Suddenly this friendly, steadying gesture became a fierce embrace. Their fingers began to unlatch buttons and unzip zippers, and their hands roamed, caressed, and fondled. They kissed with open, insistent mouths and probing tongues. It seemed to Clifford that he was two persons, one who reveled in this gasping, clutching commotion, another who stood aghast over the terrible reckoning which would surely follow. Astonishingly, he and she were making love in a standing position, their legs canted, their sweating pelvises colliding and recoiling, their heads listing dizzily. Finally, he sagged inertly, sickened by the odor of simmered garbage, and it seemed only her strong arms held him upright. Wordlessly he followed her into the apartment, and she disappeared into the bathroom and turned on the shower. He sat in a stupor at the table until it occurred to him that he wasn't obliged to wait and he shouted through the bathroom door, "I'm not coming back ever again."

His house seemed more vacant than ever before. It was as if a mortician had emptied its veins of blood. He was certain Dixie had known of his rank, sweating sin upon the instant of his committing it. It was an inconceivable violation of her trust, an unforgivable affront to her dignity. He showered but knew mere soap and water could not cleanse him. Loath to defile the commodious bed he had shared with Dixie, he bedded himself in the room formerly occupied by his son. Unfortunately he dozed rather than slept, awakening over and over from tortured dreams. In one dream he saw a line of charging Yankee soldiers; cannons roared, muskets exploded, handsome young men threw their hands upward and died. He struggled into consciousness and threw back the sheet, intent upon phoning Sheila with the news that her husband had not been killed in battle, that he was here in this house, very much alive and very much in love with her. Then her delusion broke upon him and he wept. In another dream he saw a scapegrace pair, a lecher named Clifford, a harlot named Sheila, dancing a lewd dance before the eyes of God, their buttocks bare and grotesquely inflated. He awoke and with a perfect lucidity asked himself how he had happened to sin so enormously. In his most sordid fantasies he had never supposed a man and woman could copulate while standing. Bitterly he recognized it was a knowing Eve who had shown him how the deed was accomplished.

At dawn he went onto the deck and had a glass of orange juice. After a few swallows he steadied into a desperate courage, though his palms remained clammy and sweat trickled along the hollow of his spine. A robin chirruped among a trellis of roses in a neighbor's backyard; on the lawn nearby a half dozen children lolled sound asleep in sleeping bags. He fancied God loved the bird for its unsullied song and those sleeping children for their innocence. He knew God no longer loved him. A subtle envel-

oping membrane isolated him from grace, which in this benign dawn could not otherwise have failed to bathe and
bless him. If he gestured, no one would see; if he spoke, no
one would hear. Already God fed him loneliness, the food
and drink of that dismal kingdom which the unvaliant would
inherit on Judgment Day.

After breakfast Clifford drove to his Payson store, where
he found comfort in processing invoices all morning. In the
afternoon he joined three golfing cronies on a Provo course.
By custom he paired off with George, who didn't belong to
the church. As they strolled from green to green, Clifford
confided to his friend that he had undergone an unfortunate
lapse in morals.

"You old son of bitch," George said with admiration,
"imagine you shacking up with some babe!"

"I'm in for it now," Clifford said. "They'll excommunicate me for sure."

"For hell's sake don't tell them. If you think the Five
Star General in the Sky is keeping an eye on your
unhandsome deeds, settle matters with him and leave your
bishop out of it."

George wore his cap jauntily back upon his brown pate
and mouthed a large cigar whose delectable fumes Clifford
willfully inhaled. Its fragrance reminded him that there
were meals yet to be eaten and pleasures yet to be harvested. All afternoon, tantalizing images of Sheila occurred
to him. He recalled with a refreshed desire how in the dark
garage she had countermanded his clumsy, trembling fingers and had herself loosened her dress. Yet as he and his
friends stepped onto the final green, he remembered his
communion with Gaylene and Ellie in the temple gardens.
Miraculously he struck the ball through in a single swing
and with a following putt sent it rolling into the hole. While
he leaned on a club observing his friends putt, he recalled
Sheila's words on that Sunday when he had first eaten at
her table: "I imagine there could be a kind of stark pleasure
in confessing a terrible sin. It would be such a triumph over

the appetite for respectability." With this Clifford became resolute. There was no question that he must confess and do penance as the church required. Any small chance of Dixie's forgiving his offense lay only in that direction.

During the following weeks Clifford spent long days at his stores making orders, stocking shelves, and conferring with his accountant. If he arrived home before bedtime, he watched television in the basement. He continued to sleep in his son's room. He took turns spending Sunday afternoons with the families of Ellie and Gaylene. It was his plan to confess to his daughters before he confessed to his bishop. However, as July, the month of Dixie's birthday, approached, he found himself unable to do so. In fact, a terrible deceit entered his mind. He would tell his children that his craving for nicotine had overpowered him and he had resumed smoking and for that reason couldn't go to the temple as planned. He would of course confess his adultery to his bishop and hope that his ensuing excommunication might be kept secret from his children and friends. Shortly after making this decision, on a late, lonely evening, he had a cigarette from a pack he had prophetically hidden in the ammunition drawer of his gun cabinet.

Thereafter he took particular care to smoke in the tiny office he shared with Seraphine in his Payson store, allowing butts to accumulate in jar lids on the desk. At last the offended Seraphine was goaded into speech. "It's going to have to be you who dumps those butts before they spill onto the desk because I'm sure not going to. And maybe you noticed I don't do my paperwork in here anymore. I guess I don't need to tell you that I don't know what on earth has ever come over you, Clifford. I believe you've gone crazy, quitting the filthy weed and getting yourself to the temple and then here you are back to smoking again. You just go ahead and fire me because I say it how I see it. You're just a wicked, foolish man."

Late that evening while he watched television at home he had a phone call from Gaylene. "Please, Daddy, tell me

Seraphine doesn't know what she's talking about. She says you're back to smoking. She says I can come see for myself. She claims your office is littered with cigarette butts."

"I'm so sorry, sweetheart," he said. "I've got no backbone at all. I knew it was wrong. I don't know what came over me. I just broke down and had a cigarette and now I'm back right where I was before."

"Oh, Daddy!" she cried and hung up. Her voice recalled to Clifford the bleat of a wounded doe which on a hunt long past he had approached to give a finishing shot.

Angry phone calls from his children who lived out of Utah quickly followed. "Dad," said his son Bill, who was an insurance executive in Rhode Island, "how in tarnation did you let this slip up on you? Sooner or later you'll get emphysema or lung cancer and then you'll die. Why not quit while you've still got some time left? But it's too late now to make Mom's birthday. What I want to know is what Joanne and I are going to do with these air tickets. They're the kind you can't turn back in for a refund."

"Maybe you could come on out anyhow and we could have a little family reunion."

"No way!" Bill said. "I couldn't take it. Maybe a little later we'll try to get out and see everybody, but not now. I'll try to sell the tickets to somebody. If I have to, I'll give them away."

On the following Sunday morning, while Clifford sat smoking on the deck, Ellie rang the front doorbell. After he had stood in the doorway for a while, she said, "Please let me come in, Daddy. I don't mind if you're having a cigarette."

They seated themselves in the plush chairs of the living room. "The way we've been doing things it's Gaylene's turn to have you to dinner today," Ellie said. "However, I think she doesn't expect you. So I've come to insist that you come to my house every Sunday for a while. To be truthful I don't think it's very decent of Gaylene to pout the way she does, but she'll get over it after a while, and things will get back to normal."

"No, Gaylene knows just exactly what she's doing," Clifford said. "Even though I wouldn't think of smoking in front of the kids, they can't help knowing what I'm up to. I don't think a weak-spined old man should be coming around and showing these beautiful, decent little kids a bad example. So I don't think I ought to come over to your house either, though it's awfully sweet of you to be thinking about me."

"Don't you dare say you won't come to my house," Ellie sobbed. "You're my father no matter what you do."

That afternoon he had dinner with Ellie, her husband, and their three little children, and afterward he dozed on their sofa, happily rousing from one moment to another to respond to the request of a grandchild. Late that evening the night manager of his Center Street store phoned saying she was shorthanded. Clifford drove to the store and stationed himself at the drive-through cash register. Throughout the night he fetched goods and rang up sales in a stupefied state of mind. Toward morning a van with a fishing boat in tow pulled up at a self-serve gas pump. When the driver paid, Clifford recognized him as Warren, the range botanist who was married to one of Sheila's friends.

"I'm taking my boys out for a little early fishing," Warren explained. "Speaking of going out, I don't suppose you'd be interested in coming along next Saturday on a hike over Timpanogos."

"I'm afraid I wouldn't."

"I know things have cooled off between you and Sheila, but it wouldn't hurt you to do certain friendly little things together once in a while, would it? At any rate, I think Tammy has in mind giving you a call."

When Tammy phoned the next evening, Clifford was embarrassed and void of ideas, and he numbly agreed to go along on the hike. They picked him up in Warren's van before dawn on Saturday. Sheila said hello when Clifford seated himself beside her but looked silently out the window while they drove. She wore a floppy hat, a checkered shirt, and jeans. Dan and Cora sat in the rear seat hugging one another in a demonstrative fashion. "Now don't do that here," Cora giggled.

Warren parked at the base of a ridge ascending the southern side of the mountain. On the previous evening he and Dan had parked another car at a trailhead on the northern side where the hike would terminate. The hikers strapped on packs and canteens and in the early light began to climb. There was no trail, and except where an occasional thicket of oak required a detour they kept to the barren ridge. The pitch was astonishingly steep, and they made slow, laborious progress. Sweating profusely, Clifford became alarmed over his quivering legs, gasping lungs, and pounding heart but saw no alternative to trudging steadily upward.

A carnival spirit seemed to possess the others, including Sheila, who had visibly revived. The women maintained the lead, chattering volubly and exulting in the fresh, moist scents of the morning, while Warren and Dan shouted puns and bellowed verses from a sea chantey. Once while the women rested upon an outcropping of rock, Sheila halted the approaching men with an outstretched palm. Holding aloft her arm, she recited in stentorian tones from a pocket "Othello": "I care not for thy sword, I'll make thee known, though I lost twenty lives. Help! Help, ho! Help! The Moor hath killed my mistress! Murder! Murder!" Pausing, Sheila clutched the volume to her breast, and Tammy leaped from the outcropping, scooped up stones, and heaved them at the dumfounded men, shouting, "Abusers of the defenseless! Traducers of the innocent!"

"Oh, not my Dan, no, not my Dan!" cried Cora, restraining Tammy's arm. "Sweets for the sweet," she called to her husband, blowing him a kiss. With a lordly wave Dan acknowledged his wife's devotion.

An hour later, pausing for a sandwich, they broke into couples. Though sick with fatigue, Clifford cored an apple and offered half to Sheila. "It's droll to see you and your

friends make on," he forced himself to say. "I hope I'm not
too much of an intruder. I apologize for letting Tammy talk
me into coming along."

"Don't apologize, please," said Sheila, who again seemed
pensive. "I've come along myself to humor Tammy. She thinks
you and I should get married. She believes she discerns a
great affinity for one another in us. Tammy's very good-
natured, very loving, and very naive. She fails entirely to
understand the strife between the body and the spirit. But
isn't it good that we're here together on this remarkable
mountain? We really haven't had a chance to say goodby
properly, you know. Besides, you have to see the goats.
They're nothing like domestic goats. They have shaggy white
coats and shiny black hooves, noses, and eyes."

Above them the crest of Timpanogos extended for miles
on either hand, serrated by an undulating succession of peaks
and saddles. Below them lay the valley with its glinting
lake, its grids of tiny houses and streets, its patchwork farms,
its rim of mountains.

"This beauty is deceptive," she said. "It is so vital and
so real yet so perishable. One becomes attached to it. There
is the problem."

"I agree," Clifford muttered blankly.

"May I ask how you've made your peace with Dixie?"

"I haven't," he said. "She's gone, I'm sure. I didn't see
her in the temple. Ellie said she was there; that's all. Dixie
and I were finished on the day she died. That's the way it is
for a man like me."

"And your children?"

"I'm smoking again. That's all they know. I couldn't
tell them anything more, could I?"

"No, I think not. I'm sorry you're smoking. It's so
unhealthy."

"It doesn't matter," he said. "I'm about used up anyway.
I may not make it back to town today. An old run-down
specimen like me shouldn't tackle a mountain like this."

"Oh, dear!" she said. "Shall we turn back? We could

borrow Warren's keys and let the others go on."

"I'll make it. People never have heart attacks when they expect them. Just wait for me to catch up once in a while."

She took his knife and cut a candybar, offering him half. "What are your plans for your future?"

"I have my stores to keep an eye on," he said. "I play golf with my friends. I can go to Ellie's on Sunday. From time to time I'll stop by a restaurant for lobster and French fries."

"So your life will just go on. I hope it won't seem too dreary. I find a kind of saving simplicity in dull and routine things."

His tongue labored over astonishing and unreconnoitred words. "If I hadn't been such an old and faltering man, I would have asked you to marry me."

She laced a boot, refusing to meet his glance. "Would you really have wanted to marry me?"

He toyed with the knife, a thick, many-bladed instrument which he loved for the multiple uses it could be put to. "If I were nearer your age I would ask you to marry me now." He closed the knife, took her hand, and wrapped her fingers about its handle. "I'm very fond of this knife. If I were nearer your age, I would ask you to take it and keep it as a token till we could go to a jeweler and get you a proper ring."

She turned the knife about, opening and closing its blades one by one. "I'm so deeply and wonderfully honored, and I'm very torn. I want to say yes most desperately. But where will you lead me? Where will I lead you? Aren't we like oil and vinegar? Though we occupy the same bottle, one floats above, one floats below. At one moment I was very proud to be the friend of Clifford and Dixie. I congratulated myself on my triumph over physical inclination. I was hopeful that at last I had escaped the condemnation of circling through existences like a circus pony on an endless track. Now I can only beg your forgiveness for knowing too much about your body and for allowing you to know too much about mine."

She returned the knife and strapped on her pack. "Really," she said, "we shouldn't marry, should we?" "No, it was a very silly idea."

The hikers resumed their earlier formation, women in front, men behind. They trudged in silence except for occasional exclamations over the increasing rigor of the slope. Clifford expected to discover at any moment he could no longer lift each weighted foot. He suffered an attack of vertigo in a chimney where for perhaps a hundred yards the trail ricocheted dizzily upward between parallel ribs of rock. Beyond the chimney they encountered a well-worn trail, which, angling toward a peak, bisected the vast rock-rubbled slope with geometric precision. In time they saw a golden eagle fly up. It had been feeding on a dead horse, which lay upon a stony pile fifty yards below the trail. Clifford had no explanation how a horse could have arrived at this point. When the party had passed by, the circling eagle dropped from the sky and settled again upon the carcass.

At noon the hikers arrived on the crest of Timpanogos. In the distance rose a profusion of blue mountains. Immediately at hand a sheer cliff fell away a thousand feet to the floor of a glaciated gorge. On a last high outcropping of rock teetered a hut with large, glassless windows from which the hikers scrutinized the gorge below. Leaning nonchalantly over the abyss, Sheila sang a snatch of a song. "Atta girl," shouted Warren. He named a song, and when she had finished, Tammy called for another. Sheila sang with closed eyes, her shoulders swaying, her hands circling. Her alto voice amplified and diminished strangely amid billows of wind.

Clifford believed she sang for him. The question of their marriage, he saw, was far from settled. For weeks he had imagined her sharing his bed and shower, eating breakfast at his kitchen table, sitting beside him for late TV. Now he thought of the day when he or she would die. At just this moment the eagle which had fed on the carcass of the horse spiraled upward on an eddy of mountain air. Clifford had expected that an eagle could do better than feed on rotted meat. Its golden, carrion-fed glory was a sign of the mortal condition, in which every triumph was followed by a defeat, every lull by a shock, every gift by a robbery.

It seemed to him the hut was rocking like a boat. He retreated from the structure with the elaborate caution of a man who knows he is drunk and seated himself on the side opposite the abyss. The tilted prairie of rock which the party had traversed during the preceding hours wavered unsteadily before his eyes, as if it were on metal springs and had not yet found equilibrium. He ate a handful of raisins to quiet his stomach and riveted his gaze upon the miniature cities resting on the placid floor of Utah Valley. From this distant perspective the paltriness of human affairs stood apparent. Yet he could see that, petty though they were, the cities in the valley below were a mark of godliness, an emulation on the part of their builders of God's mastery over a recalcitrant nature.

Warren and Dan seated themselves beside him and rummaged in their lunch sacks. Warren pointed out a plant whose tiny, trumpet-like blossoms lined up toward the sun in a precise vertical row; it was his opinion that the blossoms of this species had evolved in response to a single pollinator, a species of hummingbird.

"Will you lend me the keys to your van?" Clifford asked. "I've decided to go back the way we came."

"There's no sense in that," Warren protested. "It's much shorter to go down the way we planned. Also, once we get past the glacier, the trail isn't nearly as steep."

"A couple of hours ago," Clifford explained, "I asked Sheila to marry me. That was foolish of me. Luckily she turned me down. But I don't know what I'd do if she suddenly changed her mind. I'm afraid she thinks the offer is still open. I used to carry a crystal she gave me. Sometimes I could feel its heat in my hip pocket. I quit smoking and went through the temple. I threw the crystal away and now I'm smoking again. Crystals are a worse addiction than nicotine. So if you don't mind, please let me take your keys. I'm frantic to put some distance between me and Sheila."

"Let him take your keys," Dan said. "I think he's doing exactly right to stay untangled from that goofy gal."

The women seated themselves nearby and began to open their lunch sacks. They listened with wide-eyed astonishment while Warren informed them of the new arrangement.

"I'll go down with you," Sheila said to Clifford.

"No, please, you go on with the others."

"You need someone for safety's sake," she said. "What if you sprained an ankle or broke a leg?"

"I'll be all right. You go on with the others. I don't want to break up the party."

"Break up the party? You're demolishing it!" cried Tammy. "It's treason to abandon us at this point. We can't go on without you. What would be the fun of that? I thought everyone was in such a good mood. Going back by yourself! Why would you want to do that?"

"Please forgive me," Clifford said. "I didn't intend to ruin your outing. I can see it's very impolite of me to turn back. I can't explain why I should. I keep thinking about my daughters Ellie and Gaylene. They're wonderful girls. They have high expectations of me. I have a feeling I should go see Ellie and Gaylene this evening and talk over a certain matter that has been troubling me. I have a feeling I should go down this mountain the way I came up. That's all. Just a feeling."

"Well, then, we'll all just go with you," Tammy said. "We've made it to the top. That's what counts. Who cares about going down the opposite side?"

"I think he wants to go alone," said Sheila. "If he has a hunch, I think he should follow it. Intuitions are almost always correct. They guide you around unforeseen troubles."

"I have a hunch we should keep Clifford company going down this mountain," Tammy said. "I have a hunch we'll keep him from a lot of unforeseen troubles that way."

"Don't be stubborn," Warren said to his wife. "You did

a nice job getting Dan and Cora together, but you can't win 'em all. Let him go. Give up gracefully."

"Sheila and I are like oil and vinegar," Clifford said. "We don't mix very well."

"All that's needed is someone to give you a proper shaking," said Tammy. "But who am I to tell you what to do? You're a very nice man and I'm happy our paths crossed on a couple of occasions. I'm embarrassed to have been so insistent that you come on this hike. I grant you warned me fairly it wasn't a good idea. I'm a simpering fool who'd pair up every lonely couple in the world if she could."

After lunch, Tammy and Cora led off along the eastward trail, followed by their husbands. Remaining with Clifford, Sheila began a half-dozen stifled sentences. "I had rather expected more time to say goodby," she finally said, tears welling in her eyes. "But I respect your judgment in this matter. I think we're dangerous for one another. I think we ruin one another's spiritual life."

She squeezed his hand and hurried after the others. Clifford stood fast until the group had disappeared around a bend in the trail. The wind crooned in the struts which anchored the hut. Overhead the eagle carved a great slow circle. Clifford strapped on his pack and trudged down the return trail, again afflicted by the stark tilt of the mountain. He was chilling from the wind and he had a pain in the pit of his stomach.

Scarcely a hundred yards from the hut, he paused and sat on a ledge, struggling against an ignominious impulse to turn about and overtake the others. He lacked the fortitude to confront the treacherous trail, the terrifying chimney, the ubiquitous solitude. He had never seen a place to which loneliness was so indigenous as this great barren slope. Thick, palpable absences clustered here, the subtle and rarified opposites, the ghostly antitheses, of all the people he had ever loved. With astonishment he recognized he had lost the slightest hope of rejoining those who had died. He was irrevocably a creature of a lesser realm. He said a last grieving goodby to Dixie. She had made a great mistake, had suffered a tragic loss, by coupling herself to him. He prayed God would indemnify her wasted years.

He rose now and at a gasping double pace retraced the trail toward the summit. He passed the hut and hurried on after the other hikers, brazenly ignoring the trail's passage over precipitous drops. In time the trail led into the head of the glaciated gorge and within a few yards lost itself upon a vast, steep pack of permanent snow. Clifford had arrived in time to see the other hikers complete their descent of the icy plunge. Sheila, it appeared, had launched herself in an upright position, skidding, bobbing, flailing, but always miraculously keeping her feet. The others had slid in a seated position, their arms and legs serving as outriggers for braking their careening descent.

Either procedure struck Clifford as fraught with hazard. He paced back and forth upon the pass muttering in hysterical incoherence. At last a suicidal resolution came over him. He sat down and surrendered to the icy slope. Gaining momentum, he lost his seated posture, sprawled backward, and slowly cartwheeled about until his head pointed downhill. Feebly waving his arms and legs like an overturned tortoise, he zoomed down the slope, his weight riding chiefly on his pack, which provided a fortunate cushion against protruding rocks. He remained tranquil, marveling over the natural enmity of human beings toward things of the spirit, over their inability to make rational choices, over the sudden and surprising ways in which they were prone to die.

With vast amazement he realized he had come to a halt, alive and uninjured, among the other hikers at the bottom of the snowfield.

"I didn't know you were into lugeing," Warren called.

"Marvelous technique," Dan said. "Will you give me lessons?"

"Are you hurt?" Sheila said anxiously, helping him stand.

"I may have banged this elbow a little," he said, removing the shredded remains of his pack.

"Is it broken? Does it feel all right?" she asked, delicately fingering his elbow.

"I believe it's all right," he grunted. "Just a minor knock."

Tammy pulled a small wood recorder from her pack. "The world is so delirious, the world is so mad with joy!" she cried. Trilling a Renaissance tune she danced wildly around Sheila and Clifford. "Be merry, you louts," she shouted at Warren and Dan. "Sing a hymn to Hymen, god of marriage. Oh, dearly beloved, be in love forever!"

"If you would quiet this unseemly clamor, you could hear the goats," Warren said. They listened and heard a distant melodic bleating. On a high terraced cliff they saw a dozen of the shaggy white animals, some lying at rest, others afoot and grazing.

"There they are at last," Sheila breathed.

The hikers now traversed the moraine beyond the snowfield, a tossed and tumbled confusion of broken rock. Not a teaspoon of soil, not a blade of grass was anywhere visible upon its broad, jagged surface. They scrambled over boulders on their hands and knees, wobbled uncertainly on teetering stones, jammed their boots into fissures. Beyond the moraine, a snow bank extended into the water of a small emerald lake. A kid goat gamboled in the snow near the water's edge. Some yards above, a mother goat sprawled upon her side. She had a thick white pelt, a tiny pointed beard, and sharp back-curved horns. She watched with unperturbed, reflective eyes while the hikers traversed the snow bank. She quickly lost all interest and turned her gaze elsewhere. Her kid continued to frolic.

The hikers rested on the opposite shore of the lake, eating remnants of lunch and dressing blisters with protective patches. Tammy borrowed Sheila's "Othello" and read passages aloud. Warren, stretched at full length beside her, mumbled, "We're desperately civilized, don't you think, listening to the great bard here amongst the marsh marigolds and mountain goats?"

A dispute rose between Cora and Dan whether the mother goat, which still lay on her side in the snow, was ill. "Just look at her thick hide," Dan said. "If you had that shaggy hair on a July afternoon, you'd be glad to cool off on a snow bank too."

"No, somehow she doesn't seem healthy," said Cora. "Who ever heard of a wild animal letting human beings pass so close by, especially one that has a baby to protect? Did you see how dull and listless her eyes were? I know she's dying. Oh, dear, that poor kid! What will become of it?"

"The good mother goat mustn't perish," said Tammy. "Who will step forth and heal her?"

"I will," Sheila said. She walked to the edge of the water and fixed her eyes upon the opposite shore. She elevated her right arm. "Sister Eliza Goat," she intoned, "I command you to arise from your bed of affliction and walk."

Suddenly the goat heaved herself onto her front quarters and, sitting on her haunches like a dog, looked about. In a moment she got onto all fours and languorously stretched each hind leg. The hikers burst into applause and laughter. "A miracle! A miracle! A case of true healing!" Tammy shouted. The goat ambled to the edge of the snow bank, exchanged a sniff with her kid, and began to graze on the sparse mountain grass.

Sheila squatted beside Clifford. She closed the knife with which he had divided a sandwich and put it into her pack. In low, urgent tones she said, "For a long time, perhaps for centuries, I have wanted to slip my mooring and drift away on a tide and be lost forever in the ocean of the spirit. But I can't go yet. I love the world too utterly. I love you too utterly."

The hikers resumed their progress, pairing into couples and slowly allowing the distance between one couple and another to increase. The trail descended by switchbacks through a wide, heavily vegetated canyon, passing by groves of fir, thickets of maple and ash, and meadows full of lupines and daisies. Clifford followed Sheila wordlessly, listening to her stories and bits of song. He puzzled over his boundless joy. In this mood he could easily believe that God had lent his grace to unruly nature and blessed even the sinful and disobedient with some degree of consolation. He could easily believe that on a wild and holy mountain God had judged the fervent love of a natural man and woman and, finding it sufficient, had granted them to make a sacrament of their marriage.

SUNSWATH

MID-SUMMER WE VISITED HARLAN'S OLDER SISTER AND brother-in-law in Logan. Although they had raised Harlan, it was the first time I'd ever met them face to face. Harlan was suspicious about going, but when Winifred promised they'd stay off the topic of our unmarriage and irreligion, Harlan said okay. You'd have a hard time finding more tolerant and liberal Mormons, Winifred being a professor of nutrition at Utah State University and Milton being an ear, nose, and throat specialist. They bought our little boy Carter and Harlan and me swimming suits, mine at a maternity shop, and we went waterskiing and sunbathing at Bear Lake, staying overnight in their motor home, which is almost as big as a Greyhound bus. Winifred drove on the way through Logan Canyon so that Milton could play Old Maid with Carter. The canyon slopes were layered with great grey limestone cliffs.

Harlan, sitting in front with Winifred, raised his voice over the rumble of the motor home. "Rocks have essence of a sort. You can kind of communicate with them. Lately Bill Thorden and I have been working on a fence for the BLM out the other side of Hanksville. Suppose at lunchtime I'm sitting with my back to a boulder, I can feel it and it can feel me. There's a current between us."

Winifred said, "That's a pretty way to put it. Mormons

believe the earth has a soul so maybe we also believe rocks have souls."

"You don't believe anything of the kind," Harlan said.

"Don't we believe the earth has a soul?" she called back to Milton.

"Yes, that's certainly true. Yes, I think so, I think we do."

"You never spoke politely to a rock in your life," Harlan said.

"Well, I certainly respect rocks," Winifred said.

The lake was utterly blue: bright sun and drifting puffs of cloud, powerboats churning among listing sails, Milton's outdoor motorboat among them. Winifred sat on a little throne of sand, a beautiful woman of fifty-five—legs muscled and tan, belly flat, silver hair cut square. She talked about Harlan as a child. Once he had climbed a tree and couldn't get down, his tennis shoes wedged in a crotch. The fire department came with flashing lights and wailing sirens. They sent for a saw, thinking they'd have to cut off a limb. Then somebody thought of untying his shoe laces and lifting him out.

A wind was coming in directly from the lake, bringing a slow surf. Milton steered his powerboat past us, Harlan in tow on a pair of skis, crisscrossing the wake. Carter sat by Milton. They waved and we waved in return.

"When Harlan was little, did he get along with your kids?" I said.

"It would surprise you how he let Edith persecute him, considering she was two years younger. But he and Keith didn't have much conflict."

"Was he broody and black?"

"Well, no. Serious-minded, however. Has he got broody and black?"

"Quite often."

"That's just too bad."

"I apologize for us not being married," I said.

"I'm not saying a word about it. We promised."

"I'm very bitter toward the church."

"I supposed you were."

"Even if I come back in, I'll pray only to Heavenly Mother. No more prayers to Heavenly Father."

She rubbed a wrist and looked over the lake, very uneasy. Mormons think God is married — Father and Mother God. Our Mother in heaven isn't active. We aren't permitted to pray to her, so I do.

I was excommunicated the spring before I met Harlan. When I got home after my trial the lights were off and I had to let myself in. When Mom came I wasn't surprised to see Dad wasn't with her. She said he had gone out to the ranch. Of course she was crying; had been for several days.

"The informer, it turns out, was Dad. I've been cut off because Dad told the bishop," I said. "And who told Dad? You did."

She couldn't deny it. My gaunt mother in her cotton print dress, flat heels, bare legs: a religious anoretic with a barren face; a conscientious alien to self-esteem; a perpetually violated virgin. Her cheeks were grooved — shadowy little runnels carrying tears to her chin. One summer night I confessed to her that during a dismal year at Weber State I had managed to have sex with five guys. I hoped telling her would help me quit; maybe help me not be so angry.

When we left Logan and started home for Boulder, Utah, Harlan drove by a back road over a mountain named Monte Cristo. "What have you got against your sister?" I asked him. "She and Milton both seem like wonderful people. You've been hiding them from me."

"They disgust me," he said. "Talk about conspicuous consumption. Like hogs at a trough, they use up a hundred times their fair share of the world's resources."

"Winifred's doing research on cholesterol. Venison is much better for you than beef."

"Very bright, very professional, isn't she? And she believes there really was a place called the Garden of Eden. Good lord!"

Coming out of a canyon into Huntsville we saw a sign that said *monastery.* "My gosh," I said. "It's not very smart to let a bunch of monks get a toehold in Mormon country; monkhood might be catching, with no cure, like AIDS."

I made him pull in. The monastery was a big farm with quonset huts for barns, sheds, dormitories, and so on. Over the one they used for a chapel rose a cross. In another they had a retail outlet for honey, bread, eggs, and milk; also for rosaries, medallions, and books.

"What happens if a pagan buys a rosary?" I asked the monk in charge of the store. He wore a black scapular over a long white robe.

"You don't look like a pagan to me," he said, pulling out a tray of beads.

I also selected three medallions. One was in honor of Our Lady of Guadalupe. "When you convert," the monk said, weighing the enameled pendant in his palm, "you will have to make a trip to Mexico to visit her shrine."

I wandered among the book stands collecting a little armload — *The Autobiography of St. Therese of Lisieux; The Rule of St. Benedict; Of the Imitation of Christ;* some others. The monk was happy. He patted the sack into which he had slipped the rosary and medallions and books, saying, "Now you have been warned. Remember that."

"Yes, thank you for reminding me," I said. "Something like that is pretty easy to forget."

"What in hell are you doing?" Harlan whispered as we left.

"There aren't a lot of bookstores in Boulder," I said. There aren't any, of course.

"Yeah, but those books!" he said.

A month later, Winifred and Milton phoned asking if they could visit us. In the middle of the night before they came I got up to take Carter to the toilet. Harlan had been in camp with Bill Thorden all week. After I had put Carter back in bed, I went into my room and lit two candles on a little table covered with a white cloth. Midnight is when nuns and monks say matins. I wanted to pray for Harlan in a way that would do him some good. The rosary was on the table but I didn't touch it. You're supposed to say prayers while you finger the beads—ten Hail Marys for each Our Father. I had an idea Catholic prayers would be easier to say than Mormon prayers: if God listens to Catholics, who are in the wrong, why wouldn't God listen to me? My wanting to say some Hail Marys was actually very irrational. You have to understand our Heavenly Mother isn't Mary; she's truly half of God, not just the foremost of the Saints. No matter. I couldn't get past that rosary coiled on the table. Who ever heard of a Mormon lighting candles on an altar?

It being a hot night I slipped off my robe so I was naked. I would like to know somebody's true opinion about God and a naked body. I have thin cheeks and a long jaw and a broken nose (a gift from my father in my twelfth year). I'm not tall and my legs are toothpicks and I have hardly enough bottom to make a decent cushion for sitting. So imagine a pumpkin bulging below my corrugated ribs, gleaming orange-white in the candle flame, reflections of Eve and the commencement.

How do women who have quintuplets survive all the umbilicals tied into their womb like so many IV's, draining, draining, draining? I don't think I have a gift for mothering. When I first get pregnant and vomit all day I think about abortions. Speaking of umbilicals: there's one between me and Harlan. He has a lump of coal inside, bigger than his two fists, pure poison. His blood circulates around it, soaking its surface; some of the blood dies, turns yellow. It trickles through to me for dialysis. My body cleans it, takes out the particles of coal, and sends it back. I have worried for a long time about his sediment building up inside me. Calcification of the will, so to speak; depression. I've got enough of my own; I don't need his.

After breakfast I went frantically to work cleaning up our little house, not too much, just the living room, which is also our dining room and kitchen. The linoleum was littered: plastic blocks, bread crusts, dried mud, and, in a corner, a cereal bowl full of chicken droppings which Carter had harvested. He played they were eggs.

Early afternoon Winifred and Milton pulled up in their motor home; flowers emerged, he in a yellow jump suit, she in a pink dress, maroon sandals, a thin maroon belt. They had brought a gift for Carter, a truck with batteries and a remote control. Milton got down on his hands and knees and showed Carter how to operate the truck. Looking up, he said he wanted to put on a gala dinner that night in the motor home. They both marveled over the view we had through the plate glass window — across the road, the Thorden's weathered frame house with Virginia creeper climbing the rock chimney; beyond that an orchard and a couple of alfalfa fields; then red slopes dotted by solitary pines; beyond that, Boulder Mountain, smoke-blue with timber.

Later Milton and Carter went for a walk and Winifred began leafing through one of my Catholic books. Her voice was a murmuring alto, very comforting: "I'm supervising this graduate student who's a Catholic. She's researching what happens to proteins in microwave cooking."

"Catholics aren't so bad," I said. "It wouldn't be much stranger being a Catholic than being an elephant trainer."

"Oh, no. Mabel is a very, very fine person."

"Do you think God listens to Catholic prayers?"

"Oh, I would certainly think so."

"Probably not, however, if it was a Mormon saying them," I said.

Her laugh was all nerves. "Are these Harlan's?"

"Mine."

"Have you been saying Catholic prayers?"

"I've been thinking about it. When I try, I can't make enough spit to swallow."

"I wish I knew about Harlan," she said. "I would feel so much better if I knew he lived by some little shred or scrap of the gospel. Does he ever pray?"

I shook my head.

"I thought of him as my own son," she said after a while. "Though not exactly. I tried to raise him in stewardship for Mother and Father. When they were killed and he came to live with us, we told him to go on calling us Winifred and Milton; we didn't want him to forget."

"That was probably for the best."

"I have strange feelings, seeing your smock," she said. "I bore two babies. Maybe I should have had more. Though you can't go on forever."

"Nuns don't have any babies," I said. "They are married to Jesus and they call him the spouse of virgins."

She looked at our bookshelves. "You have such weighty books. You are both very intelligent. Harlan was gifted. He used to debate. Also he used to sing and paint. One of his paintings took a prize in the Utah state fair. I can't believe what has happened to him. He finished the course work for a master's in computer science and then he quit. You tell me he drives steel posts with a jackhammer. It makes me dizzy thinking about it. I had a testimony, at least I thought I had a testimony, that he would magnify himself through painting or music."

Mormons have an optical way of putting things. Does magnifying yourself mean that you use a lens to make yourself appear bigger than you really are? Or that you are bigger to start with than you appear?

After Harlan had got home and showered, we crowded into the motor home and watched the production. Winifred set paper plates and plastic glasses on a blue table cloth. Milton, wearing an apron, chopped salad, stirred sauce, and sliced French bread. Carter climbed into Harlan's lap and settled into the crook of his arm. I would be grateful if Carter didn't look so much like me: emaciated ribs, a frail chin, bulging eyes, an unhealthy skin. Milton was expounding on motor homes, chiefly to Harlan, who smiled a little and nodded slightly, not listening, his eyes gone elsewhere. Harlan has sandy hair, somewhat receded; a wispy beard, tiny ears, a delicate mouth; very handsome in a mournful way.

Our dog whined at the screen door. "Guess old dog wants some supper too," Carter said.

"I imagine," Harlan said.

"I want to hear the song about Fido."

"Not now."

"Yeah, now."

Harlan winced, hummed a pitch, sang: "Oh, I have a dog, his name is Fido, I raised him from a pup; he can sit on his back legs if I hold his front legs up."

Milton applauded. Carter said, "That's funny."

Milton said a long blessing on the food—pork chops, white grape juice that looked like wine, a chocolate cake. Carter stood on his cushion and pointed at the cake. "I want some of that."

"Hush," I said. "He's saying the blessing."

Milton said amen and things were terribly silent. I could smell dead ants.

"There's this corporation trying to put together a golf course deal out in Smithfield," Milton said, serving Carter a chop.

"We are against it," Winifred added. "We want to see Cache Valley made into a rural monument, something like the Lake District in England—the farmers and the enlightened public working together to keep Cache Valley worth visiting and living in."

"Tell me something funny," Carter commanded.

Harlan said, "I saw a flying mule the other morning. A levitated mule, an ass drifting above the earth."

"Oh, no, you never," Carter said.

"One of our mules had got himself onto a laid down trunk of a juniper, a big old one. From where I lay in my bedroll, I couldn't see anything but his neck and ears above a little tree that was in between. He looked like a floating donkey in a painting by Chagall."

"Who's he?"

"Don't bother to find out."

"I certainly have no taste for Chagall," Winifred said. "A child could paint better than he did."

While Milton sliced the cake, Winifred said, "Is there something nice we can do for you two? Something you'd let us do?" A large black fly butted and buzzed in a lamp. "Wouldn't you like to go to San Francisco for a week? And let us pay for it?"

Harlan let his squinting eyes follow the fly to another lamp.

"You could go in September or October. Or whenever you like. We'd pay for airfare and lodging and meals. Everything. And we'd love to keep Carter while you're gone. Between the two of us and the next door neighbor we could manage very fine."

Harlan said, "We couldn't do that."

"But wouldn't you love it? It would be so good for you. Or somewhere else if you don't want to go to San Francisco."

Harlan turned to me for help. "We couldn't do that, could we?"

"No," I said, "it wouldn't be right."

"So what are you making of yourself out here driving fence stakes with a jackhammer? Just what are you coming to?"

"I'm civilizing myself. So's Lora."

"Oh, fiddle," Winifred said. "You're thirty years old and you're already senile. You really are."

"We consider it an act of civilization to stay away from places like San Francisco."

"Not me," I said. "I'd just as soon go. It'd do us good to break out of here once in a while."

"To San Francisco?"

"Well, somewhere."

"We just had a trip to Logan last month," he said. "But, all right, say we raise some money and take a trip somewhere."

"We wish there was something we could do for you, some way we could help you," Winifred said.

"Don't cast us off," Milton said.

"We don't mean to cast anybody off," Harlan said. He turned back to me. "Go ahead, think up a little trip. Think of a place we ought to visit."

"We don't need a trip," I said. "What we need is to get out of here. To move."

"I thought you liked it here."

"Sure, I liked it. That was when I thought you liked it. I want to move where there aren't any cliffs."

When I went into the bathroom after tucking Carter in bed, Harlan was on the toilet. The room was so small I had to climb over his legs to get to the shower. "That was nice of Winifred and Milton, offering us a paid vacation," I said. "But I guess it's a nefarious plot to rehabilitate us."

"You're damned right it is," he said.

We lay side by side on our bed, no clothes, no sheet. "I see you've been worshipping false gods again," he said. I hadn't removed the candles and white cloth from the little table.

"I'll put it away in the morning."

"Let it stand. What do I care?"

"We need something," I said.

"We've got something."

"You talking about dying, that's what we've got." Later I said, "Shall we make love."

He scratched his beard, a grainy rasping. "Do you want to?"

"No, but if you want to I don't mind."

"I guess not," he said.

The first time we ever went into Buller's Gulch and saw the tiny ruin, Harlan was ecstatic. "In this place you can hear the past; eternity is tangible here." He sat in the clean, bright sand, legs crossed, arms folded, eyes closed. Carter lolled asleep in a packapoose on his back. I sat on a boulder and listened, hearing, as Harlan had claimed, many things in the summer silence. Audible inaudibilities.

I said, "Maybe it's God."

"Sure. You can call anything God."

"I mean God the Father. And God the Mother. Also God the Son and God the Holy Ghost."

"The Holy Christian Quadrumvirate. You are anthropomorphizing. The evidence for Christianity exists in human fantasy, not in the material world."

"So where is the evidence for anything else?"

"It's scientifically proven that all matter is unified through the laws of physics. I can hear the electrons. They exist; they buzz like bees in a blooming tree. That's God. But I can guarantee you it isn't personal."

He disappeared through the tiny door of the ruin, which stood beneath an overhanging cliff. After I had nursed Carter, I peered in. My irises expanded, slowly shaping images: creviced walls of stacked stone, bark shredding from roof poles, Harlan kneeling before a hole in the floor, in one hand a digging stick, in the other an ear of corn no more than four inches long. "It's at least eight hundred years old," he said.

After lunch, he shelled the tiny kernels and ground them on a flat rock. He carefully shook the meal into my open palm, saying, "First the meal, then the batter. A little grit makes no difference; that's how the Anasazi ate it. Every adult skull they find has severely worn molars." Taking his aluminum cup, he climbed the narrow slickrock defile we had come down, knelt at a tiny catchpool, and dipped water. Returned, he splashed a little into my palm and stirred the paste with a twig.

"Just a taste for each of us, washed down by water from a natural cistern. This way we'll know authentically how it was for the Anasazi." He dipped his finger into the paste, licked it, sipped from the cup.

He gazed away with mournful eyes. He dipped his finger again and raised his cup, saying with a mocking resonance, "Take, eat: this is my body. From this cup drink my blood, which is shed for many."

"Don't speak such words if you don't believe," I protested. "They frighten me."

"I believe in the Old Ones," he said. He offered me the cup. "This is a sacrament of the Anasazi. So that we can have their grace."

"That's not how the Anasazi would have done it," I said. "They would have added pollen to the cornmeal and scattered it to the four winds."

He pushed my hand toward my lips. "Go on, lick it clean."

"That's nothing to make fun about," I said, scraping my palm across the rock.

Toward morning when I came back from the bathroom Harlan was awake. "Lord, I wish they were gone," he said.

"They try to be nice. They love you an awful lot."

"I'm just getting goddamned frantic."

I reasoned it would be good for him to make love. If you make love you are still alive, aren't you? Of course I was just a big torpid snail in the purple dark. Where was my slim belly, my lace panties, my see-through nightie?

On the day of her consecration St. Therese of Lisieux had a vision of a mantle of snow upon a statue of the Child Jesus. Because she loved snow she knew Jesus had been thinking kindly of her. Life wasn't easy in the convent, but Therese took each hardship as a special blessing. A sloppy nun splashed dirty water on her in the washroom; she didn't try to avoid the splashes. A fidgety nun disturbed her during meditation and prayer; she didn't protest, didn't move elsewhere. As she lay dying she was haunted by an unbelieving voice that seemed to say, Dream on, you poor deluded nun, till the night of annihilation overtake you. How kind of God! How wonderful, how merciful! Every hardship was a gift that helped mortify her flesh, helped her know this world was unreal.

So I was somewhat sorry for what I was about to do. I took Harlan's hand and kissed his fingers. I stroked his shoulder, walked my fingers across his breast and over his belly, slid his hand down the outside of his leg, brought it slowly up inside his thighs. He rolled against me, kissed my lips, took my breast.

Later, we lay tangled, my leg over his, his arm under my neck, his fingers in my hair. A breeze sifted cool through the screen. Very softly, voice wavering, he sang a fragment: "Where the evening primroses are blooming, out on White Mesa so fair." He said, "You're so fine." Then hoarsely: "Three days ago I saw a primrose growing in a sandstone crevice. I lay down by it and looked close at its white petals and at its pistils dusty with golden pollen. I named it Lora."

Had he actually done that? I didn't care. Mother in Heaven, I said, don't let me let him die; I can't accept that much mortification of the flesh.

After lunch we headed over the Burr Trail in our Datsun pickup, Winifred and I in the front, Harlan, Milton, and Carter in the back. Every time I slowed for a dip or curve, dust caught up with us. I was happy to see the manful grimaces in the rearview mirror, though of course I felt guilty. I said to Winifred, "There's something to be said for polygamy. I can see some advantages in sharing a man with other women. A man can get to be quite a burden."

"Oh, I don't think so. I'm personally very thankful for the Manifesto." Later she said, "Is it quite different living with a man you aren't married to?"

"No, I don't think it's very different at all."

"Do you think it would be nice to be married?"

"Yes, it would be nice," I said. "However, I don't think we really fit. Somebody cut me out with pinking shears; my edges don't match his."

"My word. I was afraid there was something."

"He wants mothering, and I'm not a motherly person."

"Of course you are," she said.

"Well, I wish you could take him back."

"Take him back?"

"You can't, but I wish you could."

"You have your little boy," she said, "and of course another on the way. Please don't get discouraged. Milton and I, our edges didn't match up so perfectly either; we just

overlapped the torn edges and sewed ourselves together."
The tires rumbled and pounded on the corduroy road; gravel
clattered against the fenders. "Of course, when you do that
you lose some material, don't you? A bit of your self
disappears."

We parked at the head of Buller's Gulch and set the ice
chest in the shade of a pinyon. Then we hiked into the
gulch, using ancient footholds to clamber down the defile.
Milton and Winifred were astonished by the tiny ruin.

"Obviously a five-foot man would have been extraordinarily tall among the Anasazi," Milton said, his eye glued
to his camera, his finger triggering the shutter. "There, honey,
that ought to justify the science of nutrition. It just shows
what good foods have done for modern man."

We followed a trail along the side of the gulch. Pausing
at the base of a gigantic boulder we saw petroglyphs — spirals,
zigzags, circles; creatures with stick-like bodies: bears, deer,
men, women, eerie humanoid beetles. Milton jerked into
action, kneeling, craning, snapping, advancing, happily muttering, "Holy Moses, get a load of that!"

"These figures are quite rudimentary," Winifred said,
"like something four- and five-year-olds do in the nursery
school."

"But aren't they marvelous? Doesn't that look like an
ear right there?"

"Oh, darling, not an ear! Now look at this strange
creature." She pointed toward a beetleman with flaring shoulders. "I do admit you could almost imagine the stirrings of
civilization."

"I hope not," Harlan said.

"Where's an ear?" Carter said.

"It isn't an ear," I said. "It's a spiral."

"The ear is a funnel," Milton said. "You can transcribe
a spiral onto a funnel very easily."

"What do you mean, you hope not?" Winifred said to
Harlan.

"The hydrogen bomb wasn't known to the Anasazi.

Neither was direct mail advertising."

"I don't think those are things you should judge civilization by."

"You think civilization is a wheel; you think every time it goes down it comes up again. Actually civilization is a ski jump and we're racing toward a catastrophe."

Carter was tugging on Harlan's pants. "I wanna drink, Daddy."

"Everyone is entitled to their own opinion," Winifred said.

"You're a Christian, aren't you? You believe in Armageddon, don't you?"

"No, not exactly, I don't."

"Well, I'm not a Christian and I do believe in it and it can't come any too soon to suit me."

He gave Carter a drink and took his hand, continuing along the trail with Milton and the dog close behind. Winifred remained, staring after them. "That was certainly an aggressive gesture," she said. "I'm not sure what I did to deserve it."

"You don't need to take it personally. He's very cranky about the end of civilization. He'll be disappointed if it doesn't come soon."

"What on earth does he believe in then?"

"Simplicity. That's why we moved out here, so that we could simplify. This was Walden for us."

Hiking in Calf Creek one day we found a dying ewe in a little hollow. She lay on her side, neck outstretched, flanks panting; the iris of her unblinking eye was large and yellow, its pupil bottomless. From her vagina protruded the hindquarters of a dead lamb. Nearby a living firstborn lamb stood on trembling legs. Our dog advanced to the ewe, sniffed suspiciously, jumped back when her legs threshed. Her spasmic hooves had cut two arcs in the soil.

"What's the matter with her, Daddy?" Carter said.

"She's going to die. Which is the fate of all living matter. But she's going to die now."

Carter stared, his lips pouted, his little red tongue sliding in and out.

"Shall we pull the lamb?" I said.

"Not me," Harlan said. "It won't do any good anyhow. She's done for."

I tried. The ewe kicked with a fresh surge, emitting strange coughing grunts. I gave up and stood back, rubbing grit and crusted wool from my palms, saying, "It's so pitiful."

"Death is a chemical condition," Harlan said. "It has no emotion. It's a fallacy, so to speak. Think about your knees. I've had some luck with that lately. Knees are hinges, very mechanical like the hinges on a screen door. When people begin to think about cruelty and pain and suffering and death, when they begin to make something out of them, that's when they go wrong. A rock doesn't wring its hands and wail and lament."

Somewhere in my esophagus a thistle had stuck. There's a zoologist who has devised a mathematical measurement of parental attrition for the benefit of offspring; he has figured out units for measuring the increased probability of death for a parent with each altruistic gesture toward an offspring.

"I'm going to puke," Harlan said. He got onto his hands and knees and vomited; he remained so, whimpering and drooling.

"Is he going to have a baby?" Carter said.

"No, you can vomit for lots of reasons besides being pregnant," I told him.

I squatted by Harlan, hugging him, patting his back, rubbing his shoulders. "Let's be Christians again," I said.

Harlan, Carter, and Milton had left the trail and angled upward toward a high crest. Winifred and I took our time, skirting certain boulders, climbing over others, coming at last to a jagged sandstone top which fell away in a sheer drop. The land was open in all directions, scooped, carved, wrinkled: canyons, valleys, slickrock pavilions, forests of juniper and pinyon, ridges, buttes, and peaks. A cloud bank mounted in the westward sky, through which sunswaths broke.

"Unbelievable! Magnificent!" Milton was saying, hastily reloading his camera.

Harlan and Carter sat on the cliff, their feet dangling into the void.

"Please bring Carter away from the edge," I called to Harlan.

"He's all right."

"Please, I would like him back here."

"I don't wanna come, Mamma," he shouted.

"Harlan!"

"Get back there, son," he said, taking his arm.

"I don't wanna," he wailed.

Harlan helped him up and I seized his arm and pulled him away. He kicked me and I shook him. Harlan remained on the verge, hunched, feet dangling, hands flat on the rock.

Winifred took a seat close behind him, curling her legs and propping herself with an arm. She squinted against the wind and grasped at her flying hair, vexed. "Windy places seem to have their own rules," she said. "I suppose we have to submit to them without complaining." A tiny spider wandered on Harlan's shoulder. "Gracious," she said, "you're being invaded." She flicked the spider into the wind, then brushed his shoulder half a dozen times.

"Let me go," Carter said, still twisting in my grasp.

"Will you stay away from the edge?"

"No." So I clamped his neck harder and missed something Winifred said to Harlan which made him heave up his legs and pivot about to face her. I heard her say, "I can't go home and leave you like you are. What will Mother and Father say to me?"

"You expect a big confrontation with them, I suppose."

"Someday, yes. Please don't make fun of me. You know I can't believe anything else."

"No," he said, "you couldn't."

"When you first came to us, you were impossible one Sunday in sacrament meeting, wiggling and whining and picking quarrels with Edith, and I took you into the foyer, Milton staying with Keith and Edith, and I whipped you. You said, You aren't my mother, and I cried as hard as you did and said, I have to be."

"Well," Harlan said, "don't bring up sad old things like that. Think about something objective. Think about the fact that satellite orbits are in the form of a wobbling ellipsis."

"Will you come away from here, Harlan, away from Boulder, away from fence building? Will you get into something with a future? Will you marry poor Lora?"

He stared at a nearby rock, then gave it a back-handed shove. It disappeared over the edge. "What do you think?" he said to me. "Should we get married?"

I said, "I think we ought to get off this cliff."

"Why don't you go back to school?" Winifred said. "We'd help you all the way. It's no disgrace for you to accept a little help."

"Certainly not," Milton said. "You could go right on with that master's degree."

"And Lora too," Winifred added. "She could go on with her schooling if she'd like to."

"Absolutely!" Milton said.

"Where would we go?" Harlan asked me.

"Maybe Colorado State. They have a good school of environmental studies."

"Please," Winifred said.

"We'll see," he said. He swung around again, legs dangling, head bent as if he was studying the jumbled terraces far below. From the west a minor squall advanced in a canopy of clouds, stirring dust and trailing veils of mist, new sunswaths appearing in its wake. "It's very grand, isn't it?" Winifred said. "A person can feel very religious in a place like this."

He said, "There's no reason other than the peculiarities of the earth's chemical composition why a person couldn't walk up one of those sunladders."

"Yes, like Lancelot crossing a chasm on the edge of a

magical sword."

"No fantasy to it; really, authentically, if we knew how to transpose our atoms, if we knew how to suspend the electromagnetism of our bodies, we could climb a beam of light." She knelt very close behind him. "This wide, wonderful wilderness means everything to you, doesn't it?"

"I would like to wink out of it. Turn the light off, that's what I'd like to do. After all the stir and frenzy of the Big Bang, all this absurd, senseless, chaotic careening of particles through the universe, I wish somebody could reverse it, could send it back, return it to the original purity of the first great black hole. By God, that'd be a Second Coming worth talking about."

"That's very quaint, very poetical."

"Except he means it," I said. "Come on," I said to Carter, "let's go hunt for lizards."

"Hot dog!" my little boy said, starting to forgive me.

I got up at dawn the next morning, gave Carter bread and jam, and took him out to feed the chickens and the lamb. When I had settled down to milking the cow, Harlan came from the house, chest bare, feet bare, hair mussed. He picked his way carefully through the corral and sat on an upturned bucket. I went on squeezing the cow's teats, spurting milk into the rising foam.

"I didn't sleep very well," he said. "I couldn't get my mind off what Winifred and Milton want us to do. Which is go back to living on their money and learn how to be decent people again."

"You slept some," I said. "Your snoring sounded liked a hay baler."

"Anyhow, I have a plan. I see a way to go. My mind is made up."

"So what's your plan?"

"We'll tell them we've been touched; they've got through to us; we want to repent, want to change our lives, want to give ourselves a total overhaul — getting married, getting back into the church and everything. Furthermore, we want to move up to Logan and enroll in Utah State, which has a good wildlife resources college, so we can be close to home and all its wonderful influences and not be deceived and misled by the philosophies of men."

I said, "They'll know you're lying. They're not stupid."

"We won't overdo it. We'll act confused and uncertain about it all so they'll think it's for real."

"So why do it if it isn't for real?"

"I want them to be taking care of you," he said. "I've worried an enormous amount over what will become of you and Carter and the new baby. But Winifred and Milton, they're good people; they're absolutely the salt of the earth. They'll help you till you can get on your feet."

"So where are you going to be?" I asked. Suddenly I knew. "No," I said frantically, "that isn't a way out."

"That's what I want to do," he said. "It would be a great relief."

"No, I don't agree to it. Not at all. Not one little bit."

"You'll be a lot better off," he said. "You'll be a whole lot happier."

My landscape was the underside of a cow; pungent uric odor; silky Jersey hairs swimming and snaking like waterweeds through my tears.

"I want you to let me go," he pleaded. A blackbird warbled from a fencepost down the road. It said, If a person is beyond repair, it isn't a mercy to keep him on life support machines; sometimes pulling the plug is the right thing to do.

We had corn flakes and orange juice in the motor home with Winifred and Milton, who were overjoyed. She hugged and held Carter on her lap, kissing his cheek over and over, saying finally, "Phone us to tell us what day and we'll come back down for the wedding."

"Given the time of the year," said Milton, "perhaps we should act immediately to rent you an apartment. Later, if it doesn't suit you, you can move to something else."

Winifred marveled: "This couldn't have come about by

natural means. I feel so holy in this place. You might say, what poor circumstances for such a momentous event, this cramped dining nook, nothing better than orange juice for making our celebration. But, no, what a beautiful sunshiny morning, what dew on your hollyhocks, what high blue mountains, what a tranquil rural village—what a place for a memory! I won't ever forget." She was weeping.

"The Boulder ward holds sacrament meeting at eleven," Milton said. "We thought we'd attend before heading for home. Would you like to come along?"

"No," Harlan said, "not yet; later on we sure should get into that again." He looked at me. "Maybe you'd like to go. Maybe you ought to dress up Carter and go."

"I wanna go," Carter said.

"Take him," I said, "but me, I couldn't do it just yet either."

At twenty to eleven they drove away in the motor home. Seated on our steps, Harlan tossed a cobble rock from one hand to another; then he strolled across the road to the Thordens'. Although I was still in shock an idea had come to me. I got into the Datsun and headed for Escalante, where there's a tiny Catholic church visited once a week by a priest who drives from Cedar City.

An hour later I knocked on the door of a small, battered trailer. I was in luck; the priest answered. He was in shirtsleeves, his stiff collar unbuttoned and a little askew like the bumper on our pickup; he was bald, somewhat portly, sad. He held a small frying pan and a can of hash.

"Do you mind coming back?" he asked.

I said, "I need to talk to you. You can go ahead with your lunch. It won't bother me any."

He let me in and turned to a tiny gas stove. I sat down and swept crumbs from the table cloth. He was frowning, holding his head aloof from the sputtering, smoking pan. "Do you have a problem?" he said.

"What I need to know is what happens to suicides on the other side."

"Are you quite depressed?" He looked very lonely; at least I couldn't help feeling lonely for him.

"It isn't for me. It's for somebody else."

"You ought to get in touch with the authorities," he said. "I mean, with a counselor or a psychiatrist."

"There's none of that kind of people around here. Besides I don't think it would do any good. He has wanted to die for a long time."

"There's a psychiatrist who flies down to Cedar City every Wednesday for public health services. If you don't have money the state pays."

"Do you think you can keep a person alive by praying for him?" I said.

He spooned hash onto his plate and set the pan to soak in the sink. He uncorked a wine bottle and poured a glass. He sat and spread a paper napkin over his lap. "Prayer is always useful," he said. Then he crossed himself and began to eat.

"So will he go to hell if he kills himself?"

"That depends on his state of mind. When a distraught person commits suicide it isn't necessarily a mortal sin. In the opinion of the theologians most sinners of any kind don't possess enough knowledge to be damned; they go to purgatory instead. However, only God really knows."

"He wants to walk off a cliff onto a bridge of air. He wants to feel his atoms shucking off as he falls, like sparks off a space shuttle when it re-enters. He wants to dwindle and diminish till he's light as a feather and will never hit the ground but will blow away on the breeze."

He stared at me, solemnly chewing. "Do you have your own minister somewhere you might talk to?"

"No, sir. I used to be a Mormon, but they excommunicated me."

"We have a mission if you're interested."

"I couldn't be anything but a Mormon, thanks just the same. Someday I'll go back."

"Is this person devout?"

"He's very undevout."

"I'll give you the mental health service number. You'd better give them a call."

"The truth is, I want him to die. I'm tired of it all."

He divided the remaining hash with his knife.

"We're not married," I said, looking down at my belly. "We've got a boy who is three. I've stood all I can. Harlan and our little boy and now this new one inside me—I'm very, very tired. I think maybe it would be the right thing to let him go. He suffers a great deal. I don't know why. Even if you say, Look, stupid, quit suffering, he still can't do anything about it. He just goes on hurting, month in and month out."

"If you can forestall him and don't, that would be very bad," the priest said. He got up, found a pencil, and scratched a Salt Lake phone number on a card. "Call them long distance first thing in the morning. They'll help you work something out."

I took it but didn't bother looking at it.

"I'll say special prayers for both of you. Also for your little boy."

"What will God think of me if I let him go?"

"Suffering is no excuse for anybody," he said.

I stood in the street thinking, unable to go home. It's no fun watching a dead man move, hearing him talk; it's easier to walk away, to let him die of simple neglect like the deformed babies the Spartans exposed on hillsides. I drove up New Canyon, west of Escalante. The road curved and dipped, gradually rising in the trough of the canyon. At a beautiful bend of the creek I parked and got out. I was light-headed and dizzy: sun and midday heat; odor of willows and aspen; slopes textured with outcroppings, cliffs, ravines, and timber.

My eyes hunted for gnarled old trees and oddly shaped boulders. Astonishingly, they found a sheep. Across the creek stood a deserted sheep camp, a wagon domed with aluminum sheeting, stove pipe protruding. Beyond, a solitary ewe traversed a barren ridge, a stray from a herd driven to lower pasture. She ambled, meandered, paused to nibble and once to stare; yet before I was ready to give her up she disappeared over the ridge, leaving me with a vacancy, a palpable absence; a sense, perhaps, of the miraculous; also of doubt that I had seen anything at all.

A burdock plant at my feet said, Go back to your lost sheep; feed him supper.

From Thomas a Kempis are these words, these units for measuring the altruism by which parents die for their offspring, or a brother for his siblings: Thanks be to Thee, O Thou Creator and Redeemer of men, who to manifest Thy love to the whole world hast prepared a great supper, wherein Thou hast set before us to be eaten, not the typical lamb, but Thy most Holy Body and Blood, rejoicing all the faithful with this sacred banquet and inebriating them with the chalice of salvation.

It was mid-afternoon when I got home. Winifred and Milton were still there, restless and worried, unwilling to leave till I showed up. We exchanged smiles, kisses, hugs, gratitudes, talk about our wedding. They climbed into the motor home, too quickly sober; they waved from the windows, scarcely recognizing how their hope had already dwindled.

Harlan was packing for his return to camp — folding fresh sheets into his bed roll, placing flour, coffee, and canned peaches into his grub box. I helped a little, waiting for a chance. He was melancholy and lethargic, entirely gone inside himself. Carter and I went out and gathered eggs, then gave hay to the cow and pellets to the lamb. The lamb, half grown and thick-wooled, had a docked, nervous tail. When we carried it home from Calf Creek we tried to find an owner. None of the sheepmen claimed it so it was ours.

Harlan came out to milk, still moody, scarcely glancing at me as he passed through the corral gate. Carter followed him and, as he settled into milking, leaned against his shoulder and peered into the bucket.

"People learn by watching," I said. "There's hardly anything you can't learn by standing close and watching carefully. That's why in the old days they used to apprentice boys to shoemakers. They watched; then they made shoes."

"That's likely true," Harlan said.

"For example," I said, "women could bless the sacrament if somebody would let them. They've been watching for centuries and they know how."

Carter said, "I don't wanna go to Logan; I wanna stay here with the animals."

"Well, you've got to go," Harlan said.

"No," I said, "we aren't going to Logan."

"Yes, you have to."

"No matter what you do I've decided to stay here," I said.

Did you ever try to hold water in your cupped hands? Harlan could see it dribbling out and didn't know how to stop it.

"Please don't do it," I said.

"My mind is made up."

"Carter needs a daddy," I said. "I need a husband."

He frowned and mulled, white cheeked, close to shock.

"You're out-voted," I said. "If you do it, it's on your own. As for me, I will pray for you seven times a day, starting at midnight. And I will think about you every minute I'm awake. Please don't do it."

Carter and I went into the house. I put a white cloth on the kitchen table. I brought my candles from the bedroom and lit them. I took a loaf of bread from the bread case. I set out glasses and a decanter of water. I set out the Doctrine and Covenants, open to the sacramental prayers.

Harlan stood in the door, the milk bucket in hand, the dog peering between his legs. "What does that mean?"

"We can at least try it," I said.

I seated myself on the bench behind the table. He crossed the room, strained the milk at the sink, put the bottle of new milk into the refrigerator. He rinsed the bucket and the straining cloth, all the while giving me oblique glances.

He went into the bathroom, Carter following. "Will you eat with me?" I called.

He came back, drying his hands. He took in the table, the burning candles, the bread, the water, the holy book. "It violates me," he said. "It's grotesque. It's unreasonable. It's wrong."

"We don't have anything to lose."

He sat down. Carter climbed onto the chair next to him. I tore bread and gave each of us a crust. From the Doctrine and Covenants I said the blessing of the bread. I poured each a glass of water and said the blessing of the water.

"Is this all we get for supper?" Carter asked.

"It's enough," I said. He took a mouthful and chewed, then lifted his glass with both hands and gulped.

Harlan stared without seeing; he was on a faraway cliff, yearning for a sunswath. I tore a morsel from my crust. This is for him, I said to Heavenly Mother; he suffers so much; help us both to bear it.

A WAYNE COUNTY ROMANCE

AT DAWN ON AN AUGUST MONDAY, WALLACE CAME IN from feeding his hounds, put cereal to boil, and laid a blue cloth on the dining room table. He set two places with porcelain and napkins and poured milk into a small serving pitcher. He brought stems of white and lavender phlox from Zelva's garden and placed them in a vase. Then he called Zelva.

They sat opposite each other at the table and Wallace served the oatmeal. He was large, bulky, and bald. His cheeks and neck were utterly brown, and his pate, protected by a cap when he was outdoors, was an incongruous white. He took note of, but characteristically made no comment on, Zelva's failure to spread her napkin in her lap. He of course had spread his napkin, and he dipped his spoon into his oatmeal with fastidious care. Zelva had put on a robe and brushed her grey curls. She never wore cosmetics, and her face was round, plain, and friendly. Though she was stout, she kept house, tended garden, and engaged in volunteer civic activities with energy and gusto. She practiced the violin almost daily and organized excursions every winter to Salt Lake City to attend performances of the Utah Symphony and Ballet West, yet spoke always in the hyperbolic, derisive idiom of Wayne County.

He intended to ask her to let him make love to her

immediately after breakfast because at noon she would depart with a group of girls for a week in camp. He was not inhibited by any fear that she might refuse. If he were to suggest bluntly that they return to bed, she would reply good naturedly, "Well, sure, why not?" And when they had gone upstairs to the bedroom, she would strip, lie on the bed, scratch her lolling breasts, and say something nonsensical like, "Well, start your tractor and let's bale some hay." He longed, however, to ask her in an elegant way. He wanted to utter tender, solicitous words, some of which he had found in the romances he secretly read and some of which he himself had invented.

Through the window Wallace saw tiny arcs of iridescent silver at the far western end of the valley: irrigation sprinklers struck by early sun in broad green alfalfa fields. He said, "There's a sight to see, the sun on the sprinklers."

It was the only gesture toward elegance of which he was at the moment capable. On this morning as on any other, the tender, solicitous words he had called to mind seemed oily and insincere. So he blurted, "Maybe you and me could get back in bed after breakfast. I know you're going to be busy this morning, but maybe there's time for just a little quick one."

"Well, gosh, yes, if you really want to," she said. "After breakfast we'll climb back in for a little quick one."

The phone rang as they finished their toast and jelly. It was Judith Swaner pleading that Wallace immediately deliver a bunk of unplaned lumber to her ranch. "I've got a little delivery to make right now," he said to Zelva when he had hung up. "That real estate lady who bought Joiners' ranch has a construction crew waiting for some lumber."

"I'm ready to go upstairs," Zelva said. "We can do one of your little slam-bam jobs and get you on your way in ten minutes."

"I've lost my spirit for it," he said dismally. "Early morning isn't a very good time to be bulldozing around on a bed anyhow. It seems like my blood sugar hasn't got up yet.

Shall we just let it go by until you get home Saturday night?"

"Well, heck, yes, if you don't feel up to it, let's just let it go on by," Zelva agreed. "I've sure got plenty to do."

Nonetheless, he left the house remonstrating with himself. Once when he had worked in the woods for three days and nights with very little pause and she had driven up with a load of diesel fuel, she had stood in the dark with her back to a pine and hoisted her skirt and he had taken her in less than sixty seconds. He hated to concede to age, hated to admit the fire in his stove was dying down to a few banked embers.

He drove to the sawmill and with a forklift loaded a bunk of lumber onto a flatbed truck. He drove out a dusty lane to Judith Swaner's ranch where he helped a worker stack the bunk. Then, with Judith at his side, he inspected the excavation in which her basement would be built.

"My gad, if that isn't going to be some house!" he said.

"It's probably too big," she agreed. "However, it's possible that my friends will visit me here. If they do, I want them to feel spaciousness indoors as well as out."

Judith also had a house overlooking the sea in California. For nearly a decade she had sold real estate in southern Nevada and southwestern Utah. A year ago she had opened a realtor's office in Loa and had bought this Wayne County property, moved a mobile home onto it, and proceeded with the construction of a ranch for raising thoroughbreds.

She was the only woman Wallace knew who played the stock market. He was not surprised this morning to see in her hand a printout of quotations that had arrived via the modem of her computer. "You'll remember I asked you whether I should sell last week," she said. "Well, I sold, and look here, it was the right thing to do."

Wallace politely studied the sheet she thrust into his hands. "It was a good move, no question about it," he muttered. "However, me and my broker have decided I'll just ride out the drop."

He sauntered to the truck, she following and standing by while he climbed into the driver's seat. She peered through the open door, reached in a hand, and from beneath the seat retrieved a book.

"My gosh," Wallace said, "there's that book that's been missing!"

"Is this yours?" she said with astonishment. "I wouldn't have thought you'd be interested in a book like this." The book was titled *The Nursery Rhymes of England*. It had a glossy cover with a landscape of grassy hills intersected by stone fences.

"I bought it in San Francisco last year," Wallace said apologetically. "I thought maybe I could brush up a little on some nursery rhymes for my grandkids. I meant to donate the book to the county library when I had finished looking through it." He got out of the truck and took the book from her hands. He leafed through it until he came to a particular page. "To be truthful, this is the reason I bought this book," he said. "Look here at this." On the page was a photograph of a stone cross atop a modest stone shaft; beneath the photograph were a rhyme and an explanatory text. The rhyme read: "Ride a cockhorse to Banbury Cross,/ To see a fine lady upon a white horse;/ Rings on her fingers and bells on her toes,/ She shall have music wherever she goes."

"That picture," Wallace went on, "is of Banbury Cross. When I was in England during World War II, it turned out there was a town called Banbury and the town had an intersection with this cross in it. Banbury Cross is real. I saw it with my own eyes."

Judith peered over his arm. "I'm afraid I can't see anything unusual about it. I would hope you saw something more imposing than that while you were a soldier."

"Well, hell, yes, I did," he said. "I saw Westminster Abbey and Trafalgar Square, and I also saw Notre Dame and Napoleon's tomb and Cologne cathedral. One reason I remember Banbury Cross is I met a girl there. I mean, we

agreed to meet for our first date on the corner of the intersection in Banbury. That was the summer of 1945."

"Well, that explains it then," Judith said with satisfaction. "Something grand and disillusioning happened to you
at the hands of an English girl and even now you can't
quite get over it, and you have bought this book by way of
taking a sentimental journey back to the summer of 1945."

"Gosh, no," he said. "We talked off and on about getting married, but she didn't want to be a great distance
from her mother and father and they didn't relish the idea
of moving to Utah, so when it came time for me to ship
home, we just said goodby."

He halted, uncertain whether Judith could be relied
upon. She wore now, as always, a white blouse, white pants,
and oxblood loafers. Her cheeks were freckled, her hair
bobbed, her ears pierced and fixed with small gold ear-
rings.

"Gotta ramble," he said. He climbed into the truck and
replaced the book beneath the seat.

"Thanks for bringing out the lumber," she called. "You're
very much a gentleman."

"Not hardly," he said with a wave of his hand.

The mill was bustling when Wallace arrived. From
within its corrugated metal walls emerged the shriek of saws
and the thump of falling planks while outside straddletrucks
and forklifts crisscrossed the yard at breakneck speed. He
remained briefly in the truck, remembering that in early
times Banbury Cross had marked the meeting of four important roads through the English countryside.

There had been a supper of pigeon pies and ale in a
pub where yellow lamps glowed amid drifting smoke. After
they had eaten he had another mug of warm bitter ale, and
the girl snuggled wordlessly against him, her arm resting in
the crook of his. A pleasant lassitude had overtaken him
and with it, strangely, a subtle, rare exultation. It was more
than the girl's affection, more even than the fact that he
had survived almost a year of combat in France, Belgium,

and Germany. He floated upon the recognition of a startling new competence. He couldn't deny that he had stood at a crossroads in the summer of 1945. He was, he had believed, a citizen of the world. He could go anywhere, do anything, become anybody. Yet he couldn't explain why, of all the choices before him, he had determined upon the one which could scarcely be called a choice. He had gone home to Wayne County, and there he had remained.

He went into his office, where his secretary informed him of a breakdown in the woods. By radio he learned that a hydraulic pump on a log loader had malfunctioned. He copied specifications and promised the foreman the machine would be repaired by the following dawn. He phoned Seattle and ordered the part, the supplier agreeing to place it on an afternoon flight for Salt Lake. As he finished, his secretary reminded him of his regular Monday noon luncheon with the Wayne County Rotary Club. "My gad, Ada," he said, "would you please phone the fellows and tell them why I can't make it today? I've got to drive Zelva to camp, and then I'm heading to Salt Lake to pick up that part."

Wallace conveyed his wife and her girls to camp by a dusty road ascending successively through sage, juniper, and pine. The girls, perched high on the gear in the back of the truck, shouted and sang and waved the sandwiches and cartons of Gatorade of which their lunch consisted. Two fastidious girls, Beth and Gina, had elected to ride in the cab with Wallace. For a while these two conversed in quiet, earnest tones. Suddenly they broke into a squealing struggle over a bag which Beth had succeeded in unzipping. In a moment Beth triumphantly flourished lacy black bikini panties and a bra.

"That's so mean!" Gina shouted angrily, snatching the panties and bra from Beth's hands and stuffing them into her pocket. She turned large, guilt-stricken eyes on Wallace.

"Now you girls just behave and don't embarrass me," Wallace grumbled.

"If Zelva catches sight of those, she'll scalp Gina," Beth

asserted with pleasure.

"Maybe she will, maybe she won't," Wallace said. "It's none of her business what kind of underwear people put on."

He steered the truck along the corrugated road with what he hoped was a display of stolid indifference to the ripe, nubile girls at his side. He considered the fact that among the respectable people of Wayne County sensuous feminine underthings were something of a scandal. There was no question that Zelva regarded herself as guardian of the morals and good character of the girls she led in the church auxiliary. In camp she was particularly zealous to govern with a swift and preemptory justice. There were to be no pranks, no raids upon neighboring units, no midnight sorties into the forest to frighten the naive and unknowing. Nonetheless, it was certain that on a Sunday soon after camp ended Zelva would stand in church and assert her love and admiration for these girls. She would sniffle and weep and express her doubt that she had ever before encountered such an exceptional, promising group of young women. In the same meeting at least half the girls would rise in turn and in trembly voices swear that they loved Zelva more than anybody except their own mother and father and declare that there wasn't a greater example of Christian womanhood in the whole world.

The girls couldn't have guessed that on their first date in the summer of 1946 Wallace and Zelva had left a dance and driven into the junipers where they hugged and kissed and repeatedly told one another they should call it a night and go home. Instead, they had gone on and on, unhooking her bra and unbuttoning his pants and fondling one another until around three in the morning, when they had contrived to complete the deed in the cramped front seat of Wallace's old sedan. They both felt irredeemably guilty and vowed they'd never do it again, but on their next date they did, and so things went until in September Zelva informed Wallace she was pregnant. Without fanfare or much thought about alternatives, he and Zelva got the bishop to marry them, and they rented a ramshackle little house in Teasdale and settled down to married life.

Upon their arrival in the parking lot of the camp, Zelva marshalled her girls into a file of porters dutifully conveying boxes and bundles to their designated unit. Wallace assisted until Zelva dismissed him with a grateful hug. He returned to town and, exchanging the truck for Zelva's white Cadillac, departed for Salt Lake. Wallace had mixed feelings for the Cadillac. On the one hand, it had an eerie voice which admonished him to put on his seat belt and informed him of the current temperature and barometric pressure. On the other hand, it was equipped with a radiophone and an exceptionally sophisticated police radar detector. When he had passed through Loa, he turned on the detector and, despite occasional exhortations from the eerie voice, accelerated to speeds reaching ninety miles an hour on the straightaway.

Shortly after dark he stopped at the big, new home of his daughter Martha in Springville. He ate a supper of coleslaw and lasagna while holding a granddaughter on his knee. Martha still wore the black skirt and white blouse in which she had tended store during the afternoon. She and her husband owned a sportswear shop in a nearby mall, a venture which Wallace had financed without interest.

Wallace sopped up lasagna sauce with a morsel of bread, afterward contemplating the moist fingers with which he had conveyed the bread to his mouth. "I eat just like a hog," he said ruefully. He wiped his fingers on a napkin and skewered another morsel of bread with his fork, adding, "I've been thinking of taking me a correspondence course in etiquette."

"Golly, Daddy," Martha said, "that's silly. There's nothing wrong with your manners."

"When your mother and I were in Europe," he said, "we ate in some pretty fancy restaurants." For years Wallace had served on the board of the Western Forest Products

Wholesalers Association. Once he and Zelva had traveled to
an international convention on forest products in Switzer-
land. Afterward they had taken a two-week tour of the
continent.

"There was this restaurant in Paris," Wallace went on,
"where the waiter wore a uniform and stood by stiff as a
statue and if you let yourself raise your eyebrows half an
inch he was right there asking if *monsieur* and *madame*
were in need of anything." Wallace stood and placed his
granddaughter in his chair. "Here, Cathy, you play like you're
me and grandma, and I'll play like I'm that waiter."

He folded a dishcloth neatly and draped it over his fore-
arm and stood stiffly at attention behind the chair. When
Cathy swung about to look at him, he bowed slightly.
"Peerhaps *Madame* weeshes a leetle more grumbledydoo
weeth her feesh." He turned Cathy toward the table. "Now,
Cathy, you're Zelva, so you lean across the table where I'm
supposed to be sitting and you whisper, 'What in hell is
grumbledydoo?' "

"Oh, Daddy, you're a character!" Martha burst out.

Wallace took Cathy on his knee again and cut into a
piece of carrot cake Martha had placed before him. "It has
weighed on me lately," he said, "and made me somewhat
depressed that I have never, not once in our entire marriage, told Zelva I love her. I got that trait from my old
daddy. Father would have rather had his tongue jerked out
than say something personal." He stroked Cathy's hair and
went on in a voice expressing both shame and defiance.
"For some reason I'm kind of scared lately. People keep telling me I ought to retire while I've got my health. It's very
strange the way I feel. I'm at an intersection, and I don't
know whether I ought to turn right or left or maybe just go
straight on through."

"You don't have to tell Mamma you love her," Martha
said. "She knows you do."

Wallace arrived at a terminal of the Salt Lake airport a
little after eleven. A young woman in the manager's office

confirmed that the part had arrived from Seattle. As she drove him along a corridor on an electric cart, her blouse gaped, revealing the lacy cup of her bra. She unlocked a door and went in search of the part while Wallace stood, hands in pockets, observing the straggling ranks of travelers entering and leaving a concourse. The loudspeaker announced the final loading of a Boeing 727 whose sleek, cylindrical body and gracefully canted tail Wallace could see through a window. A couple hurried by. The man wore a handsome suit and sported stylishly coifed grey hair. On his arm was a woman, easily thirty years his junior, possessed of extra-ordinarily beautiful legs.

For a moment Wallace fancied himself with such a woman on his arm. He pondered whether a knowing tailor might not transform him into a credible person of the city. He judged his most insuperable defect to be not his bulging belly or dangling arms but his irretrievably bald pate around which bristled an insignificant rim of clipped hair. The obvious repair, a toupee, struck him as a despicable deception, a foppish prosthesis which would only invite ridicule and shame. He longed to be made into a new man. As for the fresh, novel, virgin setting of his transformation, it could be any of the great coastal cities, San Diego, Los Angeles, San Francisco, Portland, or Seattle, where, if he were not content to live on interest and dividends, he could surely flourish as a broker of lumber.

Wallace arrived in Bicknell well before dawn, got one of his mechanics out of bed, and delivered the part into his hands. Satisfied that the loader would be operating by the time its crew reported for work, he went home, fed his hounds, and went to bed. Two hours later his wrist alarm awakened him. He shaved, had breakfast, and drove to the county library in Loa, it being his duty to substitute for Zelva as driver of the bookmobile. When he had served as county commissioner, Wallace had donated a van to the library for a bookmobile. The next group of commissioners had decided the county couldn't afford a driver, whereupon

Zelva had volunteered to drive it one day a week.

Mrs. Crofts, the librarian, accosted Wallace on the library steps. An emaciated septuagenarian, Mrs. Crofts towered like an ancient pine draped in an ill-fitting suit of navy blue. "While our patrons inevitably prefer books of the lighter sort," she lectured Wallace, "you should be persistent about suggesting alternatives from our shelf of classics. Would you please be particularly alert when Mrs. Schnieblom borrows her usual quota of romances? You might suggest that she take along *Wuthering Heights*, too. I was proud of Zelva last week for having persuaded Mrs. Schnieblom to borrow *The Scarlet Letter*. Anticipating she will return the book today, I have jotted down on your clipboard several questions you might ask her. I would caution against your improvising your own questions unless you have read the book recently. Just rely on my little promptings, and I think you will find yourself getting along very nicely."

"Yes, ma'am, I will do my best," Wallace declared.

Mrs. Crofts called his attention to several books ordered by interlibrary loan. Among them was a book on walrus tusk carvings of the Eskimos which Wallace was to deliver to Judith Swaner. It also happened, surprisingly, that Judith had phoned that very morning asking to borrow a book on English nursery rhymes which she had said Wallace intended to donate to the library. Wallace again felt obliged to apologize for having such a book, it being an aberration on the part of a Wayne County man to have an interest in trifling topics. However, he abruptly broke off in the middle of his explanation, recognizing, with a new kind of embarrassment, that Mrs. Crofts did not consider his interest an impropriety. When he assured her that he would indeed donate his book, she rewarded him with, if not a smile, at least a visible relenting of the vertical lines of her weathered face.

The itinerary of the bookmobile included brief stops at a number of ranches and longer stays in the villages of Fremont, Torrey, Teasdale, and Grover. Most of the patrons were elementary school children working for a reading award to be made when school reconvened in the autumn. Repeatedly the children roused Wallace from the fitful naps into which, benumbed by his all-night drive, he sank. Adult visitors, most of them wishing only to converse, also interrupted his naps. For example, at the mercantile in Teasdale where Wallace waited for an appointed thirty minutes, four elderly loafers in back-tilted chairs solicited his opinion as to whether deer hunting should be allowed in nearby Capitol Reef National Monument.

At mid-afternoon Wallace parked the van in the shade of a giant cottonwood at a crossroads near a cluster of ranches. All day he had slowly fallen behind schedule. Waiting were close to a dozen children, some of whom were the offspring of a polygamist and his wives.

"I'll bet you didn't think I was going to make it," Wallace said as he opened the rear doors and allowed the children to crowd inside. "I'll bet you thought I'd driven off the road and wrecked the bookmobile in a wash."

"Naw," said a boy, "Zelva told us you'd be the driver today. She said you'd be late. We knew you'd get here sooner or later."

A polygamist girl soon presented herself to Wallace with a book about Billy Goat Gruff and a fierce troll who guarded a bridge. Scarcely six, she wore a white smock over a long-sleeved gingham dress.

"You aren't going to check out just one book, are you?" Wallace protested. "It'll be a whole week before this vehicle makes it back."

"Just one," she politely demurred. The other polygamist children now stood behind her, each holding a single book.

"My gad," Wallace burst out, "how are you going to grow up and become lawyers and engineers and airplane pilots if you don't read more than one book a week? You don't want to be nothing but an old Wayne County hog grunting in the mud and mire, do you?"

"This is all we're allowed," said one of the oldest.

"Daddy says too much of a good thing is worse than none at all," said another.

As the last child departed, a woman appeared, trudging across a fallow field with an armful of books. It was Mrs. Schnieblom, who delivered books into Wallace's hands wordlessly and with averted eyes. She removed her shoes, revealing black, bulbous toes, and climbed into the van's interior where she knelt before a shelf of novels.

As Mrs. Crofts had predicted, the books Mrs. Schnieblom returned consisted of a half dozen romances and a copy of *The Scarlet Letter*. Clipboard in hand, Wallace began to recite Mrs. Crofts's questions, first asking whether Mrs. Schnieblom had enjoyed the book and then, after she had thrown him a puzzled glance, asking whether she could point out the symbolic meanings of the scarlet A. She stared at him incredulously for a moment, then cast her eyes about the van as if measuring the possibility of a hasty exit.

"I'm just reading what it says here," Wallace blurted in exasperation. "You don't have to stare at me like you thought I was a person who didn't have good sense. Mrs. Crofts thought you might like to have a literary discussion about this book. Here, dammit, just take this sheet and see for yourself all the nice, thought-provoking questions she put down."

"Have you read that book?" Mrs. Schneiblom asked belligerently. "I thought when Hester and Arthur met in the woods and decided to run away together things had taken a turn for the better. But they hadn't; things just got worse. I didn't think it was right to make Hester wear that letter in the first place, and I don't think you ought to write a book about that kind of thing."

Wallace slunk away and seated himself beneath the cottonwood. His back pressed uncomfortably into the corrugations of the trunk, and his half-mesmerized mind eddied eccentrically between sleep and wakefulness. He leafed slowly through one of the romances Mrs. Schnieblom had returned. He paused upon a passage about a gentleman and a lady who strolled through a wooded park on a starry night. Beyond the wooded park was a brilliantly lit mansion from which emerged gay voices and the dignified tones of a chamber orchestra. The couple paused beneath a giant oak and the gentleman took the lady's hand. He reviewed the reasons why he could not allow himself to fall in love with her. She was a married woman and had children, and even though her husband was, as far as Wallace could infer from his allusions, a negligent, womanizing cad, the gentleman respected the institution of marriage. Divorce and remarriage were furthermore out of the question because he was essentially a pauper. A London architect, he was paying off the damages from the collapse of a public building designed by an unscrupulous partner. The couple wept and embraced and whispered goodby. "I will never forget you," the architect murmured, "and I will forever hold your name in veneration." Wallace also wept despite the consoling fact that over half the novel remained, making it probable that this couple would yet find their way to a blissful union.

Soon Wallace recorded Mrs. Schnieblom's latest selection of romances and watched while she climbed through a barbed wire fence and plodded away across the fallow field. From the rear Mrs. Schnieblom resembled an ambulatory bag of onions. Wallace reluctantly acknowledged that she reminded him of his mother. It was not that his mother had possessed Mrs. Schnieblom's affinity for slovenliness and disarray. To the contrary, his mother had habitually shampooed her hair with yucca root, clad her frail body in carefully mended, hand-laundered shifts, and scrubbed plank floors with unstinting vigor. What she had in common with Mrs. Schnieblom was a chronic condition of negligible expectation. She had raised her family of four boys and three girls in a four-room shanty, depending on the infertile acres of her husband's farm for sustenance. She had disposed of milk, eggs, and vegetables enough for the table but only rarely of any surplus which might, if markets were propitious, be converted into cash, clothing, and amenities.

Wallace's father had been neither unfaithful nor tyrannical and by conscientious labor had earned, as it were, the dearth which afflicted his wife. His single demonstrable gift was for silence, an unfortunate fact for his wife, who, Wallace would later conclude, valued words more than money.

There had been no library in Wayne County, and therefore no books, during the days of Wallace's growing up, but there had been movies, a fund-raising provision of the Bicknell church. It being a religious duty, even the impoverished Rucklesteads purchased a family pass. Without fail on Saturday evening, summer and winter, the entire family cheerfully transported itself the three miles to town, sometimes by wagon, more often by foot. There were times when, following the first showing, Wallace's father and most of the children went home while his mother and a selected child or two remained to see the movie a second time. The memory of these twice-seen movies led Wallace to believe, as he pondered Mrs. Schnieblom and her weekly diet of romances, that his mother too had yearned and pined for a gentleman lover.

It was only as he parked the bookmobile behind the library in Loa that Wallace remembered his obligation to deliver the book on Eskimo carvings to Judith Swaner. He therefore carried it to her ranch in the Cadillac, bringing with it his book on English nursery rhymes, which he retrieved from beneath the seat of the flatbed truck as he passed by the mill in Bicknell. Judith greeted him on the deck of the mobile home in which she was temporarily quartered. She seemed genuinely distressed that he had disarranged his evening for her sake. There was no inconvenience to himself, he assured her; his wife being in camp, his evening was unscheduled.

"I don't suppose you'd stay for dinner," she promptly said. He having mulled the impropriety of accepting the invitation a moment too long, she said, "You will stay then. I'm so glad!"

She explained that her housekeeper was absent and without apology enlisted Wallace in the preparation of the meal. Wallace set the deck table with porcelain and silver and helped at the kitchen counter by cutting a tossed salad. He found himself inordinately pleased by Judith's features, whose disproportion had troubled him on earlier occasions: her bobbed, shingled hair, her uneven nose and hollow cheeks, her shoulders, spectrally thin and clad as always in a white blouse of fine texture.

He now felt bold enough to ask why she had wanted the book on English nursery rhymes.

"I was afraid you would want to know that," she said. "I can't pretend it was anything other than my curiosity about you. I apologize for invading your privacy."

"I don't see how it could harm me," he said.

"It's very odd how I couldn't get Banbury Cross off my mind yesterday after you had told me about meeting that English girl there. I don't think you realize just how exceptional a person you are. I really have no right to conjecture about your personal life, but of course I hope you'll become my friend. When a person moves into a new place, she can't only build a new house and stables and fences. She has to build new friendships too."

"You bet we'll be friends," he said. She smiled winsomely and, having shifted a stirring spoon, put out a hand, which he shook.

Shortly they seated themselves at the table on the open deck. It seemed to Wallace a rare splendor ruled everywhere: a fresh, moist breeze eddied from the fields, swallows darted in the translucent sky, the sinking sun cast a rosy alpenglow upon the parapets of Boulder Mountain. Besides the salad the meal consisted of broiled chops, asparagus tips under cheese sauce, and a white wine. Anxiously he tried to manage his knife and fork with finesse and to chew his food with cautious deliberation. Unnerved equally by the wine, from which he usually abstained, and by the extraordinary beauty of the oncoming night, he disciplined himself to listen intently to Judith's words and, when it was his turn to speak, to quit himself with good sense.

Soon he found himself narrating his unfortunate attempt to implement Mrs. Croft's plan for elevating Mrs. Schnieblom's tastes. Abandoned by her husband, Mrs. Schnieblom had, he explained, raised three children by means of county welfare and her own few acres of alfalfa and corn.

"My goodness!" Judith said. "And this woman reads romances!"

"Three or four a week. Year round she's the bookmobile's most dependable customer."

"It's very difficult for me to conceive of that," Judith went on. "Does she keep herself ready for a real-life romance? Does she do her hair and put on makeup?"

"Good gosh, no," he said.

"I'm impressed with Mrs. Crofts," Judith said. "Isn't that encouraging to think Wayne County has a librarian of that caliber? Mrs. Schnieblom obviously needs drastic changes in her life. She shouldn't be reading romances. She should move to Salt Lake or Las Vegas and get into an employment rehabilitation program. I have no patience at all with reading romances. There must be five hundred new love novels published every year. If I had my way, I'd burn every one of them."

"I read a romance today," Wallace said. "That is, I browsed in one for a while."

"And you found it rather silly, I would imagine."

"Well, no," he said, "it seemed like a pretty good story." Although he had hoped to sound disputatious and aggressive, his voice emerged contrite and apologetic.

"Tell me, then, what you like about romances."

He hesitated, finding it suddenly necessary to scratch his thigh. Fields, fences, other familiar forms were rapidly becoming indistinct in the twilight. A dim wash of silver diluted the western sky. Overhead a jostling crowd of stars gathered.

"This is incredible!" she remonstrated. "First I find you

reading books about English nursery rhymes and then I discover you reading romances."

"What I like about romances," he said, "is that things get said that should be said. If people are in love they ought to say so."

"It seems natural to me for adolescents to believe in love. It doesn't seem natural for you to believe in it."

"You're probably right," he conceded. "It's a waste of time to read romances. A man ought to read Westerns."

"You mustn't let me badger you," she said. "You really don't hold up your end of an argument very well, you know. My God, if you really were in love with somebody, it would be less than human not to express the fact with proper words. My point is that love is a terribly fickle emotion. When you consider that it has to occur simultaneously in two people, I think you are much better off, much less likely to suffer disappointment, if you discipline yourself to ignore it."

She lit candles and refilled his goblet with wine. He felt befuddled and foolish and unfortunately obliged to say something wise and entertaining. For no clear reasons, he recounted an incident he had observed between his father and mother when he had been fifteen or sixteen. He had blundered upon them seated at the table with pages torn from the Montgomery Ward catalog between them.

"I didn't have to take a second look to know those pages were the corset and brassiere section which Mother always tore out before she put the catalog in the privy to be used for toilet paper because she didn't want those pictures of women in their underwear to tempt her boys to commit the solitary vice, as they used to call it. But of course I was familiar with those torn-out pages because you can't keep anything private in a house as cramped as ours was."

"And did they truly tempt you to commit the solitary vice?"

He sat in embarrassed silence.

"I suppose that isn't to be discussed."

"Please not," he pleaded.

"You astonish me over and over!" she laughed. "There is something so utterly and soberly innocent about you."

"I'm anything but innocent," he protested.

"But coming back to your mother and father sitting there with the pages torn from the catalog between them. It couldn't be possible, could it, that your mother had to ask permission to buy a bra or a corset?"

"Well, yes, it's possible," he said. "But I don't think it was exactly permission that Mother was after. I think she was proselyting him."

"Proselyting him?"

"I think she was trying to convince him that he should want her to wear something delicate and dainty. This of course is the conclusion I have come to in later years. At the moment all I knew was that my presence was a terrible embarrassment to them."

"Why should her wearing something delicate and dainty take any convincing?"

Again he was silent.

"You come from a line of male Victorians, don't you?" she said.

"I don't think my father failed to do what comes natural when it's late at night and all the lights are out and the kids are sound asleep and you know that good-hearted woman lying there beside you with nothing on but a nightgown won't say no."

"The way you describe it is almost pornographic."

"I didn't mean it to be. What I'm trying to say is that my mother wanted to be hugged and kissed, she wanted to be unbuttoned and looked at, she wanted to be praised and made over. She wanted sweet words, and my poor father didn't have any to give."

Wallace finished his wine with a gulp, ashamed to have trespassed so candidly upon the lives of his parents. "Shall we take a walk?" he asked.

They left the deck and navigated cautiously among the looming silhouettes of a backhoe, a pile of excavated earth, and a stack of bricks. They paused at a corner of the newly poured foundation and briefly discussed the progress of Judith's house. They went on, following a faintly visible dirt road leading into the fields.

They came to a bridge over an irrigation ditch. "I'm afraid I'm a little drunk," Wallace said. "I can't handle much wine." Judith gave him a hand. When they had crossed the bridge, they continued hand in hand until they came to a gate. Windrows of drying hay descended a field in dark parallel lines. Crickets chirruped everywhere.

"You have a house overlooking the sea in California," he said.

"That's true," she replied.

"You behave as if you haven't thought of California for weeks," he went on. "For you Wayne County is a new life. For you it's a novelty and an adventure to live in Wayne County. For me, Wayne County is not a novelty or an adventure. I've never had a house on the sea. I'm puked on Wayne County. It bores me. It has always bored me. It hasn't bored me just a little. It has bored me high as a mountain, deep as a canyon."

"I think I can understand that," she said.

"I want to leave Wayne County," he said. "I want to leave Utah. I want to leave it now. I'm sixty-five. I don't have a whole hell of a lot of time left."

He was frightened by what he had said. He turned and cast a glance toward the distant driveway where he had parked the Cadillac. The candles on the deck made tiny twin points of yellow light. Judith stood close before him, a waiting, passive shadow. He took her hand and said, "I will always venerate your memory." He dropped her hand and groaned. "I'm sorry that sounds so phony. I read it in a book. I don't know what else to say."

She put her arms around his neck and pulled herself against his body. "Don't say anything at all," she pleaded. "This is so ironic. A romance is exactly what I didn't want.

They always blow up, and when they do, there's no middle ground."

He gripped her slight body with long encircling arms, and she murmured, "It feels so good to have you hold me."

She gave him a fierce final hug and took his hand and they returned along the road. When they reached the steps of the deck, she faced him, saying, "I couldn't be a man's mistress. I'd have to have him to myself. If this doesn't work out, I hope we'll still be friends. I really, really hope we'll still be friends."

Reluctantly conceding that he was in no condition to drive, Wallace accepted Judith's offer of a bed on the cushions of her dinette. He awoke before dawn from a nightmare. In a part of his troubled dream he had seen himself in a business suit trading in the pit of the commodities exchange in Chicago. In another part, he had been a calf roper at a rodeo. A chute opened and out came not a calf but a Brahman bull. Instantly the bull became a giant brown bear saturated from head to tail with the green diarrhea of cattle. With a malevolent lunge the bear disemboweled Wallace's screaming horse. Still befuddled and uncertain as to what had transpired on the previous evening, Wallace pulled on his pants and laced his shoes in desperate haste. If anyone at all discovered the white Cadillac in Judith's driveway—her construction crew who would arrive soon after daylight or ranchers who shared her lane—the scandal would pump through every vein and capillary of Wayne County in less than a day.

It was barely daylight when Wallace parked the Cadillac in his own driveway. Dreading to enter the empty house, he went first to his hounds in the backyard. He hadn't run a trail in three years, and as he approached the kennel this morning, as on any other, the hounds bayed and whirled in an ungainly frenzy. The brindle bitch leaped upon him when he entered her pen, placing her front paws on his chest and slavering her tongue across his chin. "Aren't you a sweetheart! What a lady! What a lady!" he said, hugging her

tightly and waltzing her round and round in a staggering
dance. He halted, warding off her drooling tongue with a
back-turned hand and staring into her amber eyes. He could
now clearly recall the events of the previous evening, and
with both relief and disappointment he recognized that he
had not made love to Judith. He remembered her slender
body and the alto intonations of her voice. Without exacting
earnest money, she had granted him an option on herself;
without his asking, she had conceded him time and grace to
ponder whether or not he wanted to take her.

After breakfast Wallace went to the mill and prepared
a bid on a tract of timber on the Dixie National Forest. At
mid-morning he received a radio call from Jerry Wanlass,
an undertaker from Richfield. At that very moment a
graveside service was in progress for a Mrs. Irene Dorby
who had lived most of her adult life in Sevier County and
had been brought home for burial in Bicknell cemetery. Re-
markably, the corpse had weighed in on the mortuary scales
at five hundred forty-three pounds. A crisis lay in the fact
that a backhoe operator at the cemetery, overawed by the
dimensions of the deceased, had dug what Jerry described
as a bomb crater rather than a grave, a pit so wide that it
would not accommodate the conventional scaffolding for lowering a coffin into its final repose. Jerry therefore wondered
whether Wallace might not have a crane at the mill which
he would volunteer for the latter purpose.

"You're in luck," Wallace said. "It so happens I do have
an old boom loader that we use for a backup to the new
hydraulic ones."

The only man Wallace could spare for the expedition
was himself, of course. The ponderous machine — a cab and
a boom resting upon the chassis of an ancient truck — rolled
slowly along the highway, wallowing and listing like a sail-
ing vessel in a heavy sea and digressing in ominous tacks
from left to right and right to left, requiring Wallace to
make strenuous corrections in the steering wheel.

At the cemetery Wallace backed the truck through a

crowd of mourners and halted at the edge of the crater-like grave. He climbed into the crane, started its diesel, and swung the boom around. He spun out cable until Jerry could hook it to a harness encircling the giant hardwood coffin. He pulled a lever and the coffin rose. He released the lever and for a frantic moment the coffin continued to rise. It stopped near the top of the boom, a great rectangular pendulum swinging heavily five yards above the earth. Wallace pulled another lever and the coffin plummeted. He clutched the first lever wildly and the coffin halted abruptly only inches from the pit. Instantly, while the boom shuddered and shook and the truck swayed, the coffin began another precipitous rise. Wallace frantically released the lever and again the coffin came to an airy, swinging rest at the top of the boom. The diesel engine putted imperturbably. Wallace climbed from the cab.

"For hell's sake, bring it down easy," Jerry said.

"I guess I don't know how," Wallace said. "This is a tetchy machine."

"Just bring it down any old way and we'll drag it into that pit somehow or other by manpower."

"I can't risk it," Wallace said. "One more try and I'll drop that coffin so hard it'll break open and then where'll we be? I've got to get Sidney over here from the mill. He knows how to operate this loader."

Wallace walked through the crowd giving his apologies. "It don't matter any," a corpulent man assured him. "This is actually kind of an interesting experience. It's curious figuring out what's going to happen next."

By means of the radio in Jerry's hearse Wallace explained his predicament to Ada at the mill. Following an unnerving silence Ada said, "I see three trucks lined up at the pond. Don't you want to wait till Sidney gets them unloaded?"

"My gad, Ada," he croaked, "I've always been a good boss, haven't I? I've always said good morning in a cheerful way, and I've let you have days off with pay so you could take care of your sick grandkids. Now, please, Ada, for once in your life move your little fanny. I've run that coffin up the boom and everybody's waiting for me to get it back down, but I can't make the loader function, so there it floats like a flag on a flagpole. I want Sidney here in fifteen minutes flat, and if he isn't, you're fired."

Ada arrived with a crew within the allotted time, and Sidney climbed into the crane and expertly lowered the coffin into the grave. With a limp wave of his hand, Sidney gave an indifferent recognition to the applause which burst from the onlooking mourners. In the meantime Wallace had edged disconsolately to the rear of the group. His ignominy seemed complete. The drivers of the trucks waiting at the mill pond had elected to ride along with Ada and Sidney, and a half dozen citizens from town had appeared, apparently informed by a perverse telepathy that an extraordinary spectacle awaited at the cemetery. Shortly a relative of the deceased pronounced a prayer over the coffin in the open pit, and the funeral was formally at an end. Without a word to Wallace, Ada gathered Sidney and the truck drivers and drove away. The mourners stood about conversing in small clusters, gradually dispersing to their automobiles with much handshaking and hugging. Wallace climbed into the truck on which the crane rested and cranked the engine, which to his great chagrin refused to start. While he waited for a ride with Jerry, he meandered about the cemetery, arriving at last at the graves of his father and mother.

Wallace seated himself on his father's gravestone and planted his hands on his knees. A hot noon sun baked the barren soil of the cemetery. It was shameful, Wallace was thinking, that the city fathers had refused to install a sprinkling system and plant green grass in their cemetery; it was even more shameful that the most wealthy citizen of Bicknell had failed to promote the planting with a liberal donation. Wallace imagined himself apologizing to his mother for this negligence and also the unseemly levitations of Mrs. Dorby's coffin. "That was so awful," he said to his mother, "me hoisting her up for a quarter hour. I never saw anything worse happen at a funeral in all my life. It'll probably show up in the *Wayne County Gazette*. I know I should have had better sense than to think I could manage that loader. I'm truly sorry."

Soon Jerry joined him, saying he was ready to depart. In no seeming hurry, Jerry cocked first one foot and then the other on a nearby stone and made some attempt to brush away the red dust which covered his shoes and pant legs. "I'm always glad to see where people's folks are buried," Jerry said. "It's uncanny how much I can tell about people just by being around their grave. It's like you can smell car exhaust after the car has driven away."

"I've got a little matter I'm going to talk over with you," Wallace said. "You being an undertaker, you know how to keep a tight lip."

"Well, that's true," Jerry said with interest. "When you tidy up the dead, you see a lot of sights that won't bear talking about."

"I've been married to Zelva forty-two years," Wallace said.

"I would have guessed it to be about that. She's a wonderful lady."

"What I want to tell you is, don't be surprised if you hear I'm walking out on Zelva," Wallace blurted.

"Well, my golly!"

"The problem is she and I have run out of things to say to each other. She and I go down to the cafe Friday nights, and she orders a hamburger steak and I get me a chop, and we sit and chew our food and look glum and stare out the window at the cars on the highway. So I'm going away to California. I'm going to sell the mill and logging operation, and I'll give Zelva her half of everything. I hope she'll know how to manage it."

"I confess this kind of rocks me," Jerry said. "It isn't every day you hear news like this."

Wallace rose from his father's gravestone and dusted the seat of his pants. "I never planned to stay in Wayne

County all my life. It just slipped up on me. I know I'm pretty old to be starting over, but by God, Jerry, it's now or never."

Late in the afternoon Wallace drove his pickup into his backyard and threw in a load of sawed juniper for Zelva's campfire. He would drive to camp and spend the night, having promised to take a turn at providing the discreet masculine presence upon which church authorities insisted as a precaution against the rowdy male visitors who had harassed encampments in earlier years. Each night a pair of responsible men from a nearby town occupied a tent modestly sequestered from the tents of the women and girls. Though it had been his duty to secure a companion, Wallace had neglected to do so in large part because his single presence would be more tolerable to Zelva, who resented this regulation. When he had told her he had volunteered to take a turn at sitting guard, as he had foolishly called it, she had bridled with anger, saying, "Thirty women and three hundred girls couldn't possible look out for themselves, could they? Any stupid guard who comes anywhere near my area gets to clean out the latrine pit."

When Wallace arrived in camp, Zelva greeted him with an affectionate peck on the cheek and told him that the girls expected him to join them for supper. Beth and Gina helped him transport the juniper in a pushcart between the parking lot and the tenting site. The hauling completed, Wallace seized a double bitted ax and split wood with an excessive vigor. He noted that the encircling pines were festooned with crepe paper stringers and balloons; between two trunks stretched a banner blatantly declaring occupants of this site to be the "Bicknell Bummers." The girls, busying themselves with the preparation of supper, exchanged a loud banter. Beyond this site, hidden in thickets of pine, were twenty-five or thirty other units similarly swarming with girls. There was, Wallace sensed, an exquisite disjuncture in his presence amid such a ubiquitous femininity. He was an earwig in an antheap, a roach in a beehive.

Wallace gave a block of juniper a vindictive blow, sending its two halves tumbling in opposite directions. Gina scooped up one of the halves and tossed it onto a pile. She had paused to ask whether he had noted their sideshow tent. Standing somewhat apart was a large tent bearing a sign: "Mme Zelva's Folies Bergeres Straight from Paree Freaks Marvels Prodigies." It was, Gina explained, an exhibition the girls had arranged, for which they charged girls from other units an admission of a quarter.

"It'd cost you more than a quarter to see it," Gina said. "You can go in for a dollar."

"Oh, no, not a man!" another girl shrieked.

"Hush your mouth!" Gina commanded. "It won't bother him any."

Wallace looked at Zelva, who smiled and shrugged her shoulders. He gave Gina a dollar, pushed aside a flap, and entered. On a couple of benches was a hodgepodge of displays: polliwogs swimming placidly in jars, a rusty bucksaw blade, a coyote skull, a candy box full of elk droppings, and, in a bottle, a tiny transparent scorpion someone had found beneath a rock. But of greater interest, tacked upon the wall of the tent like animal pelts, were Gina's black lacy bikini panties and bra and, beneath them, a white, well-worn bra that Wallace recognized as Zelva's. The ample cups of Zelva's bra had been tightly inflated with balloons.

When Wallace emerged, the girls broke into hysterical laughter. "So what do you think?" Zelva asked. "Is it worth a dollar?"

"You bet," he said. "It's plumb eye-opening. You ought to go on the road with this show. It'd be a killer in New York and Boston." Strangely, he no longer felt like an intruder and alien.

After supper the girls trooped to an amphitheater on a nearby hillside for a variety show. Bringing up the rear, Wallace and Zelva had time for a brief conversation.

"So you've come up to protect us from the rapists and robbers," Zelva said. "Where's your partner?"

"I tried to find somebody to come along with me," Wallace lied. "It seemed like everybody I asked had big commitments somewhere else."

"You should've had a big commitment somewhere else yourself. The truth is we don't need you."

"I know you don't need me," he said. "Don't worry about seeing any more of me. I'll slip away when this show's over. I'm going to throw down my pad in the back of my pickup in the parking lot. I wouldn't sleep in that tent out there on the edge of camp for a hundred dollars. Tents give me the fantods. Anyhow, when it gets daylight, I'm gone. I'll get breakfast in town."

"You could go home now, you know."

"I know it," he said, "but I'm not going to."

Wallace followed Zelva into the glare of a bonfire at the base of the amphitheater. A host of feminine faces, glinting with reflected flames, rose in tiers against the hillside. Wallace circled upward, gratefully finding an obscure seat on the topmost tier. The variety show proceeded with a hilarious commotion, a sheet of plywood serving as a miniature stage beside the fire. There were skits, songs, and dances, among the latter a clog performed by two Bicknell girls to Zelva's accompaniment. Zelva fiddled with unstinting vigor, and the girls danced with a paradoxical mixture of lethargy and motion, their bodies inertly afloat above the loose-jointed clop of their feet. The final performance of the evening was Zelva alone on her violin playing a solemn fragment from an opera. Wallace could have doubted that the woman below, flickeringly illuminated by a dying fire, was his wife had the notes of her instrument not emerged with such an elegiac clarity. An immense melancholy grew upon him. All day he had distracted himself by imagining the adventures of establishing a brokerage in San Francisco or Los Angeles and by fantasizing scenes from a blossoming intimacy with Judith. Now, however, as he confronted the imminent necessity of informing Zelva that their marriage was at an end, those pleasant imaginings seemed fatuous and insubstantial. He attended, it seemed, a second funeral. The girls and women in whose midst he sat, their happy chatter hushed by the haunting tones of the violin, had unwittingly joined in a grieving farewell to Zelva.

When she had finished, Wallace left his seat and made an uncertain progress uphill through a dark stand of aspens. Soon he emerged upon a road and followed it to the parking lot where his pickup stood. He threw down a pad in the back of the pickup, unrolled a sleeping bag, undressed, and zipped himself into the bag. Taking no comfort from the cool, pine-scented air nor from the extraordinary luminescence of the sky, he pondered returning to the mill where he could grind away the disconsolate night in neglected paper work. In time, however, he slept, awaking at a late hour to a bizarre memory of his father and mother and a dog named Jack.

Jack had distinguished himself among the family's dogs by possessing mismatched irises — one brown, the other milky white — and, even more notably, by surviving to old age. Wallace had returned from his military service to find the ancient dog suffering from arthritic joints. Discussions had been going on between his father and mother, his father invariably promising to shoot the ailing creature and just as invariably procrastinating. There was no explaining why Wallace should have recalled these events so vividly unless he found in them a parallel with his present circumstances, unless, that is, he likened Zelva to Jack and himself to his timid, procrastinating father. He had to admit that it was uncertain whether he had the courage to say goodby to Zelva. There was no one to approve of his going, certainly not Zelva, who would weep and fulminate and despair, nor his children, nor those hundreds of friends who thought of him, not as an individual but as an indispensable component of an amiable entity known as Wallace and Zelva.

Wallace slept again and awoke with a terrified start, aware that someone stood at the tailgate of the pickup. With relief he recognized it was Zelva, who, having spoken, opened the tailgate and seated herself.

"My gosh," he said, "what time is it?"

"It's three-thirty. I woke up a little while ago worried, and when I remembered you were up here, I felt better. So I came up to apologize for sounding ungrateful about you driving out here and having an uncomfortable night just so the rest of us could sleep more secure."

"It's not so uncomfortable," he said. "I've managed to sleep some."

She circled a palm over his bald pate. "Good gracious, feel that mosquito bite! Doesn't it itch?"

"It does now you've mentioned it," he said.

She bent over him and briefly pressed her cheek against his, murmuring, "Do you want to hoe my garden?"

"Good grief," he said, "do you mean right now?"

"You bet," she said. "I felt like I hadn't done right by you when we didn't get back to bed Monday morning."

"Hell almighty, Zelva," he said frantically, "there are three hundred girls down there in those trees."

"They're nothing to worry about at this hour. They're out cold. You can count on it."

He was unnerved by his instant ardor for her proposition. He had relied upon the weary indifference with which he ordinarily contemplated Zelva's plump buttocks, thick waist, and sagging breasts. Now, at this crucial moment when it seemed his new identity, his second chance at life, was at stake, he slipped, almost consciously, into an evasive vacillation over the question whether it was ethical to make love with a spouse one had decided to abandon.

"I guess this isn't a very good time and place," Zelva conceded. She had, however, begun to unlace her shoes. "You won't mind me crawling in with you for a little bit and warming up, will you? I didn't think to bring along my jacket."

"We couldn't begin to get both of us in this bag,"

he said.

"Unzip it and throw it over us like a quilt," she said.

He could not of course refuse her plea for simple shelter. After a considerable getting up and down and shifting and turning, they lay face to face on the narrow pad with an arm thrown over one another and the open bag pulled loosely over their bodies. She inquired how Wallace's week was going and exclaimed sympathetically while he narrated his sortie with the bookmobile and his misadventure with the coffin of Mrs. Dorby. In the meantime Wallace soberly noted the enormous comfort he took from the warm press of her thighs and belly and from her light fingerings of his neck and ear. With difficulty he fought down a menacing impulse to allow his own insatiable hands to resume, like cattle returning to meadows in the spring, their happy meanderings over her familiar body.

"Maybe you remember my folks' old dog Jack," he said by way of evasion. "During that summer before you and I got married, Jack had got so old he couldn't do anything but suffer. One evening Mom came out of the house with the .22 and shoved it into Dad's hands and said, 'Shoot him right now.' Dad tried but he couldn't, and Mom said something unkind and grabbed the gun back and put it to her shoulder, and, lord, Zelva, I thought she'd pull the trigger because Mom could chop the head off a chicken for Sunday dinner without batting an eye. But Jack raised his head and howled because he knew, dogs always know, what was coming next, and, my gad, Mom began to tremble like she had a fever and she turned around and disappeared into the house."

So long as he could hear his own drawling bass voice Wallace could persuade himself that his courage and resolve had not deserted him. But when this anecdote had exhausted itself, he could think only of how, during that summer when he had observed the foregoing incident, he and Zelva had unwittingly, in the front seat of a car, forged a marriage from uncircumspect disrobings and acrobatic copulations.

"It seems a scandal the way you and I were behaving that summer," he said.

"Oh, poop, it wasn't any scandal!" she said with a clipped finality.

A sickle moon, barely risen, shone indistinctly through the spires of dark, shaggy firs. The indiscretion of Zelva's recent proposition, the stark impropriety of making love amidst hundreds of sleeping innocents, had returned to Wallace. "Oh, jeez," he said in a final expiring tone of protest. An utter incontinence came over him, and he became erect.

"I think you want me," Zelva whispered.

When they had finished making love, they again lay face to face with an arm thrown over one another. Wallace mulled the deceitfulness of tactile experience, the willingness, that is, of his roving hands to persuade him, in contradiction of what his eyes for many years had too clearly discerned, that this woman who lay pressed against him in the dark had neither aged nor deteriorated but was young, virginal, and ripe with promise and expectation.

"Are you crying" Zelva asked in astonishment.

"Maybe a little," he admitted.

"What's the matter, sweetheart?" she said, hugging him tightly.

He could only go on with the story of his father and mother and Jack. "It boggles my mind to remember that Dad and Mom scraped together four dollars and hauled Jack to the veterinarian in Richfield and paid him to put the old dog away with a shot of some kind or other, and they brought Jack home to bury him on the place. We all sat down to a supper of bread and milk, and I never saw the family, especially the little kids, look glummer in my whole life, knowing poor old Jack, who had been with us fifteen or sixteen years, was lying dead out in the back seat of the car and the next morning we'd have to dig a hole and cover him up."

"Golly," Zelva said, "do you still feel bad over that?"

"Not exactly because when I went out at dawn to milk the cows, there was Jack sitting on his haunches on the back stoop, his tail wagging pitifully, like he hoped we had finished with all this mean business of trying to put him away. Of course, I woke Mom and Dad, and the kids came boiling out of the house too, and, my gosh, it was a celebration because we were all so glad he was still alive. So the folks kept him in the house all winter and cleaned up the messes he made just like he was a human being and, thank God, the next summer he died quick and easy of his own accord. So sometimes things turn out all right in this world, don't they?"

"That's the truth," Zelva murmured.

"I believe it was seeing Dad's and Mom's graves today that has made me sad," Wallace said.

His sadness had settled, like a cold, deep into his lungs. He had remembered his mother kneeling on the stoop hugging the resurrected Jack and on her shoulder his father's hand. By virtue of that hand on that shoulder, giving the lie as it did to his mother's dissatisfaction and his father's ineptitude, Wallace had surrendered to his birth and breeding, to that couple who had loved him first and best and to this woman whose fingers at this instant languidly traced the contours of his ear.

"I apologize for never having any sweet words for you," he said. "It seems like I'd rather die than say something fancy."

"Who wants fancy words?" she said. She emerged from the bed and pulled on her clothes, then sat on the tailgate and laced her shoes, muttering, "It's getting light in the east. I'd better hustle."

"I was also thinking," he said, "I couldn't ever leave you, no matter what."

"Of course you couldn't," she said. "I couldn't leave you either." She gave his bald head a final caress and strode away across the parking lot.

He raised up on an elbow and followed her dark, diminishing form. Now he sobbed violently, relieved that his unsettling impulse toward other climates had been confronted and quelled yet astonished that the road he had followed from Banbury Cross led to no other place than a grave in Wayne County.

NIGHT SOIL

A NARROW STRIP ALONG THE EDGE OF THE BED WAS
for Pickett, who in the summer slept in his clothes on top of
the covers. At the bottom center was a spot for Vincent, his
dog. The rest of the bed was stacked with magazines, westerns, and the scriptures, in which, it being Sunday morning, he had read about the Crucifixion. "Them sons of
bitches," he said to Vincent. "They didn't have no more
sense than to go ahead and do it. I'd have told Pilate where
to put it if I'd've been one of them."

"Sure you would've," Vincent replied sarcastically. "You
stand up for what's right every time, no question about it."
Actually Pickett said this in behalf of Vincent, who lay on
his back, his front paws dangling limp on his ribs, his collie
muzzle ajar, his hound ears unfurled.

Pickett got off the bed and, having only one leg, hopped
across the room, using chair backs and the table for bal-
ance. He set on coffee and when it boiled he spilled dog
biscuits onto the table for Vincent and set out Twinkies for
himself. "Pull up and eat," he said.

Vincent climbed onto a chair, sniffed the biscuits, and
climbed off. "You persnickity coyote," Pickett said. He took
in half a Twinkie with a single bite. "How come," he said,
after a gulp of scalded coffee, "they didn't have no better
sense than to crucify him? Now that takes the cake for

stupidity, don't it? Didn't they have no beans at all?"

"How come? I'll tell you how come," he answered for Vincent. "If you have two buckets, and one of them is right and the other is wrong, which one is full and which one is empty? Ha! In this old world, ain't it the truth? The bucket of wrong is plumb full."

"That's putting it just about right," he grudgingly conceded to Vincent. "I couldn't have said it much better myself."

Pickett decided to strap on his artificial leg and hike up to the cemetery to visit the grave of his real leg, which had been amputated because of gangrene. He didn't have any other folks to visit because his brothers and sisters and his grown children and his grandchildren and even his wife, who had got tired of his cranky moods and shiftless ways, all lived in the cities—Provo, Salt Lake, Ogden, and such. He unzipped his coveralls and dropped them around his ankle. His body was stringy and lightly scratched, as if God had handwritten it with a thin cursive nib: a warped shin, a taught thigh, a bent spigot of a penis set in a parsley patch, hollow buttocks, a wrinkled little belly, gaunt ox-bow ribs, sloping shoulders, jawbones rounded like boomerangs, gullied cheeks, hair sprouted silver-grey like dandelions gone to seed. He puckered, grimaced, and groaned while he strapped on the leg: a morsel of plastic thigh, hinged to another stiff plastic piece consisting of knee, calf, ankle, and foot; all the color of canned salmon that has dried on a plate all day.

He went out, Vincent following. He was nothing but a squatter, living in the kitchen of a derelict house on a dead block where barns and sheds were in ruin and cheatgrass had taken over gardens and driveways. He crossed the street and passed along a live block where untrimmed lawns and green drooping elms fronted the houses. He lurched rather than walked, catapulting his artificial leg ahead, locking the knee, vaulting up and over. He crossed another street and went by the church, from which a hymn eddied: "Oh, dearly, dearly, has he loved! And we must love him too, and trust in his redeeming blood, and try his works to do." Pickett paused, tried to hum a bit, then said to Vincent, "We ain't going into the pool hall today, feller. We're going to show some respect for the Lord's crucifixion."

Then he boiled up with wrath, remembering the bishop, who last winter in the big freeze had said, "Hell, no, Pickett, you can't have any welfare coal; when was the last time I seen you in church?"; also, in the spring: "If you can't buy irrigation shares at market price, you don't get any water; anyhow, you can't call that little patch you're scratching in a garden"; furthermore, last week: "Word is, Pickett, you been messing around up at Pansy's house; trying to get yourself excommunicated, is that what you're trying to do?" Pickett bent over the church lawn, stopped up his right nostril, and with a loud honk blew out the contents of the left. "So much for you, Delbert," he said. "However, that don't matter none," he told Vincent as they resumed their march. "We ain't going into that pool hall even if Delbert is a turkey's ass."

He crossed the highway, the only paved street in town, and angled across a vacant lot, aiming to pass unnoticed by the rear of the pool hall. Unluckily, Dan Hernstead stood on the back porch. "Aren't you coming in?" he asked.

"It wouldn't edify you or me neither," Pickett said.

"Get off it, man. Let's shoot some pool."

"Can't do it. I promised Vincent here I wasn't going to break the Sabbath."

"You can't let me down for a flimsy reason like that," Dan protested.

"It isn't hardly worth the trouble playing pool all morning when the winner doesn't get more than one bottle of beer."

"Okay, dammit, we'll raise the stakes. The loser buys the winner a bottle of beer for every game he's ahead."

"I think maybe I should come in then," Pickett said. "It'll more or less ruin your day off if somebody doesn't shoot some pool with you."

Inside Pickett and Dan selected cues from a rack and began chalking the tips. Jorley Waggs was at the grill behind the counter, back turned, fixing breakfast for Edwin and June Shurtleff, who had come in from their ranch.

"Howdy do," Jorley called. A couple of lumpy wrinkles sat at the base of his head as if his scalp and his neck had been laid out by different survey crews with nobody bothering to reconcile the overlapping boundaries. Dan broke the rack and the clicking of colliding balls filled the room. He picked off the one and two balls before missing the three. Pickett sighted down his cue and leaned across the table, his artificial leg cocked outward like a derrick.

"You ain't going to make that one," Edwin observed.

"Sure I will," Pickett said. "The Holy Ghost tells my cue ball where to go." The cue ball bounced off a side, angled behind the six, bounced off another side, careened between the thirteen and the nine, and knocked the three into the corner pocket.

"Every time," Dan said, shaking his head mournfully. He dug a nailful of snuff from a shiny can and stuffed it into his cheek. Edwin and June began eating their hotcakes and sausages. Edwin was a miniature rising to five foot four in his cowboy boots and his high crowned Stetson. June, clad in a calico dress, had frizzy curls, wrists thick as a wrestler's, and little balconies of fat hugging her chin.

"So what's your opinion on hydroponic tomatoes?" Edwin said to Jorley, who had begun to wash dishes.

Pickett answered. "I favor Sandridge Reds. They slice better."

"Hydroponic means the way they was raised," Edwin snorted, swinging around on his stool. "They raise them in rocks instead of soil. In water with chemicals added."

"It might be I'd favor them, then," Pickett said. "That farm I had back in the fifties was nothing but rocks; if I'd have known about them kind of tomatoes, I might've raised a lot out there. Never raised nothing else to speak of, that's for sure."

"I've sure ate worse sausages," Edwin said, swinging back to Jorley. "These hot cakes are something extra too."

"How's things at the mine?" Pickett asked Dan.

"We're busting out coal like nobody's business. Been setting a new record every two or three weeks."

"You don't get no sunburn down there in the pit, I guess," Pickett said. "Probably a real pretty place to work if you like black."

"Boys on the evening shift found another fossil last week. This here geologist from Salt Lake City came down and picked it up; said it was one of them amphibians. Cross between a fish and a lizard, more or less. Granddaddy of the toad, though about thirty times bigger; head the size of a washbasin, body maybe four foot long. Like a big salamander."

"Why do you suppose God would make a salamander four foot long?" June asked.

"Beats me," Dan said. "When you get God figured out, let me know."

"I imagine God didn't make it," Pickett interjected. "I imagine it just grew when he wasn't paying attention."

"Boys, thanks to Junie here," Edwin said, "we have had us a one hundred percent calf crop out on the ranch for the last three years running."

"I hope you aren't going to ruin my breakfast talking about that," June said.

"Honor is paid where merit is due. Two things Junie does all by herself, me being nothing but a consultant, is artificial insemination and calf pulling."

"Now, Edwin, that isn't anything to be talking about in mixed company."

"That's true. However, it isn't everybody that gets a hundred percent calf crop. Not by a damn sight."

"If you've just got to go into that, I'm going to the powder room," June said, sliding off the stool. She glanced at her watch. "Go on and get it over with so I can finish my breakfast." She disappeared into the ladies' room and slammed the door.

"Don't tell me you make your little lady breed your cows," Pickett said.

"Make her? She insists on it. She doesn't want me fooling around putting a glass tube up a cow's culvert. It'd be indecent. Something like adultery, in fact."

"Well, that's so," Pickett said. "You could sure look at it that way."

"She gets every one of our cows familied up. Talk about low overhead. We don't keep any bulls. Haven't done for five years. Also she had our boy Arnold bring down one of them special comealongs from Salt Lake, all rigged up with a nylon strap, which she slips over the calf's head and winches it out. Slick as grease. We keep our cows in the front pasture come calving time. June keeps an eye on every one. Haven't had no losses in three years. One hundred percent calf crop."

June put her head out the door. "Come on back, honeybunch," Edwin said tenderly. "I've finished."

Pickett gazed out the window while he chalked the cue tip. "I saw Bishop Delbert P. Wheatley's new Buick over at the church," he said. "Looks like he's prospering."

"Right there's the reason why I ain't baptized," Edwin said. "Can't be God's church if it's run by cheats like him."

"That isn't no reason," June protested. "It isn't his church. Besides that, you had plenty of chances to get baptized before they made him bishop."

"For crying out loud, Junie, don't you go siding with them and let them do my temple work after I'm dead. I ain't baptized now and I don't want to be baptized then neither."

"I had me a dream about Delbert," Pickett said. "One night in vision I saw me and him in the Celestial Kingdom."

"I imagine you did, all right," Jorley said.

"No fooling. There I was in the Celestial Kingdom and it was time to go to the bathroom and all they had was an old-fashioned privy. I went in and peered down the hole and who did I see bogged down in that privy pit but Delbert himself. I backed out and looked up at the Angel Moroni, and I says, 'Brother Moroni, I can't go to the bathroom in that privy because a feller I knew in mortality, Delbert Wheatley, is in there mired up to his neck; did you know that?' 'Sure, I knew he was in there,' Moroni says; 'now you just go ahead and relieve yourself according to custom.' 'Oh, no, I couldn't do that,' I says. 'You bet you could,' Moroni says; 'all your life he done it on you and now it's your turn to give a little back.' "

Edwin, Jorely, and Dan burst into guffaws. June said, "Well, if that isn't a filthy story."

A couple of hours later Pickett lurched up the street swinging a burlap bag lumpy with bottles of beer. At the edge of town he halted under a weeping willow on a ditch bank. Opening a bottle, he said hello to a red and white heifer on the other side of a nearby fence. He lowered himself, took off his shoe, anchored his artificial leg across the ditch like a cantilever, and dipped his real foot into the cool, muddy water. Vincent plunged through the ditch, shook off a great shower, and rolled in the hot dust of the street. "Damn you," Pickett said in Vincent's voice. "Yes, you, Pickett Inglebar, damn your soul to hell. Telling that rotten dirty story on Delbert; soiling the holy precincts of the Other Side with privy talk; crucifying the Savior afresh with your filthy fancies."

"I know, I know," Pickett replied gloomily. "I ain't got no excuse, none at all."

By the time he had finished a third beer, two boys, perhaps six and eight, came along the street. They stopped when they saw Pickett's foot in the water. "Why don't you put that other leg into the ditch?" the bigger suggested.

"You want to see it?" Pickett said, drawing back and pulling up his pant leg. The boys jumped the ditch and bent over the leg, the older saying, "That's neato."

"It don't have any hair," observed the other.

"Do you boys know how to make bottle horses?" Pickett said. "Course not. Gotta play with Transformers nowadays, ain't you? Gotta have little airplanes that really fly and trucks that run on batteries. Nevertheless, I'm going to show you how to make bottle horses. See that binder twine hung up in the fence down there? Go fetch a piece." With his pocketknife he cut loops and lengths of twine and whittled twigs, fashioning collars, traces, and doubletrees, linking a pair of bottles with a network of twine. "There," he said, "don't those look like horses? Now you take them home and hitch them to something with wheels and you've got yourself an old-fashioned outfit — horses, harnesses, and gear."

He raised a finger and said, "Boys, leave tobacco, coffee, and beer alone; don't use profane language; go to church regular; be respectful of your mother. Don't pay no mind to the fact I drunk these bottles empty. Do as I say, not as I do." He knocked hard on his artificial leg. "That leg ain't neither flesh nor blood; it don't eat and drink; it's a shackle God has locked onto a wicked man, boys."

As they went on, the older carrying the harnessed bottles, Pickett peered into the remaining bottle. "Suffering succotash," he said, "I was afraid so." In empty beer bottles, the amber kind, especially when sun broke through them, he saw visions. As clear as day he saw his little girl Jenny in a flaring starched dress, hair tidied for Sunday school. He peered again and, sure enough, he saw himself too, dressed decently in a white shirt and tie and possessed of two good legs, lifting Jenny, then hugging her. He lay back in the dust and cast his eyes overhead toward the heifer, whose muzzle protruded between strands of barbed wire. "Now isn't it wrong to love one of your kids more than another?" he said to the heifer. "First time I ever saw her, she no bigger than a plucked chicken, she wanted to melt right into my armpit. But she has forgot her old daddy now. She is growed up, has moved to Salt Lake City, has kids of her own."

"What did you do to make her forget you?" the heifer

said. "Tell me that, will you?"

"Yeah, what didn't I do?" he agreed meekly, tossing the empty bottle into the ditch. "But they do grow up, no matter what."

He dunked his bag and went up a side road, bottles clinking, his artificial leg thunking. The road, mounting steadily toward a looming mountain, radiated noon heat. Sweat beaded on his forehead; his lungs labored hoarsely. He could see Pansy's house, its paint faded and peeling, its yard littered by cartons and cans. "Vincent," he said, "I make a sacred pledge, a holy promise. I'm not going in no matter if her moron brother ain't home. Do you hear me now? Do you back me up? I gotta know right now before she spots me."

"I hear you," Vincent replied. "I'm holding my breath for you; I'm clenching my teeth; I'm puckering my sphincter. Keep going. I'm right behind you."

Pickett clattered past, staring stalwartly forward. A voice called, "Pickett, aren't you going to say hello?" She stood at the corner of the house, the Venus of the cemetery road: rubber irrigation boots and a soiled dress latched by three buttons, two others missing; a long face, gat teeth, black and grey hair tied into a snarled ponytail. "Won't you help me?" she pleaded. "My privy is busted."

He went in the gate, followed her to the backyard, and stood, arms akimbo, surveying the destruction. "Holy Moses," he said, "looks like the Ruskies nuked it." Shattered boards from the little hut, which had been wrenched from its moorings over a pit, were strewn for thirty yards up the hill.

"Me and Wendell both had a hand in it," she explained, referring to her half-witted brother. "We got in a quarrel last evening whether we were going to watch 'Love Boat' or 'Dallas.' He called me a cow elk. I tore into him with the bread knife and he holed up in the toilet. I saw blue blazes, Pickett; I went off my rocker. I grabbed the ax and chopped him out. He couldn't quite get all the way through one of the splits I made. Dragged the privy with him. Left pieces half way up the hill."

Pickett peered down through the seat, which had remained intact on the plank floor. "That pit is full, Pansy. Time to dig another."

"I know," she said mournfully.

"Why don't you scatter ashes down there? It looks worse than a mess of stewed prunes. Don't smell sweet neither."

"Where'd I get ashes? We run off butane."

"Well, let's see if we can patch it together."

He and Pansy assembled the pieces over the pit and while she held them in place he tacked them together with scab boards. Then he marked a spot where she could have Wendell dig a new pit. "When he gets it done I'll make you another hut," he said.

"Oh, Pickett, you're so good to me. Do you want to come in for some SpaghettiO's?"

"Maybe just for a bite. I can't stay long."

When he had finished eating, Pickett pushed his chair away from the table, stretched out his legs and folded his hands over his belly. He could have gone to sleep. "Don't you want to marry me?" Pansy said. "Don't we get along real good? You could get a divorce."

"Fat chance. Myra is spiteful and mean. She'll do any little thing she can do to get back on me for treating her so rotten."

"You never treated her rotten," Pansy said. She had taken off her rubber boots and now, with a leg cocked over a knee, groomed a toenail.

"Besides, I can't stomach Wendell," Pickett said.

"Oh, you can't, can't you? And I just fed that mealy-mouth dog of yours a can of SpaghettiO's!"

"A half can," Pickett said indignantly, heaving himself up. "Come on, Vincent, it's clear we ain't wanted here."

"You sure ain't."

But when he had got to the door and looked back piteously, she rushed to him and they hugged and kissed and apologized. "Oh, Pickett," she crooned, "let's get on the bed."

He rolled his eyes upward and silently spoke to Vincent, "I can't bear it, feller. Honest to God, it's more than mortal flesh and blood can bear."

"You jelly-boned badger," Vincent said, "I ain't got no respect for you whatsoever. Not one danged inch."

"You haven't had a bath in a while," Pansy said, wrinkling her nose.

"No, ma'am, I haven't, that's true."

She put a washpan of water on a burner. "Strip off and I'll wash you."

She brought him a pillow case to wear like a diaper because he was too modest to have her see his privates. He dropped his coveralls, unstrapped his leg, and stood clutching the pillow case with one hand and gripping a chair back with the other, his gullied face morose, his scarlet stump pulsing. She soaped his back and belly and armpits and wiped off the lather with a washcloth. "Time for your dainties," she said, laying the soap and cloth on the table within his reach. "My back is turned. I won't peek, I promise."

When he was through she said, "Look at me, Pickett!" She stood stripped before him: pudgy knees, dimpled thighs, billowing buttocks, narrow shoulders, bulbous breasts.

"Am I pretty?"

"Oh, lord, just like a sunrise," he said.

Afterwards, they lounged against the headboard, each with an arm around the other, drinking beer slowly, coughing and belching and gazing at the motes adrift in the afternoon sunlight. Pickett peered into his empty bottle. He saw foamy bubbles stretching like cobwebs between slick glass walls; he saw an amber glow like a moon about to rise over the horizon. "Don't begrudge the back side of things," he said.

"Oh, I never do," she said hastily.

"For example, take your privy pit, which is foul with stink. I'm lying here thinking, Ain't Pansy and Wendell ate many a fine meal; ain't they been hungry to eat and they ate. You laughed many a time, had many a fine thing happen. And you left a bit of all that pleasure in that privy, didn't you? It ain't a pit full of mire and mess. It's a picture album; it's a museum; it's your grandmother's trunk full of wonderful old things out of the past."

"Gosh, Pickett, are you crazy?"

"No," he said, "don't begrudge poor things."

He peered into the bottle and wasn't surprised to see himself and Myra and all their children at a picnic ground up the canyon. Clear water rushed over black rocks in the nearby creek. A fire smoked through the grates of the firebox over which the kids scorched wienies on peeled willows. Myra waddled about the picnic table, spreading ketchup and mustard on buns and pouring orange punch. Her waist rocked, her forearms quivered, every inch of her as soft and giving as an innertube just ready to collapse.

"Nobody but a porcupine could drive off a woman like her," he said silently to Vincent, who all this time had been sleeping in the corner.

The dog replied, "Yeah, sure thing, you bet your boots, you weasel, spending your mother-in-law's pension check on a big night out in Price! Holy mackerel, ain't you got no conscience at all!"

He peered into the bottle and saw a four-foot salamander with yellow splotches over slimy grey skin. He put the bottle onto his belly for a moment, then peered again. The salamander had slithered about and had shoved its thick catfish lips close to the neck of the bottle. He threw the bottle to the floor. Shivering, he slid down from the headboard and pulled up the sheet. "I got a chill," he said. "Mid-summer flu, I expect."

Pansy slid down beside him, got him to roll onto his side, cuddled herself into the bend of his buttocks and the crook of his knee. She kneaded his poor thin shoulders and caressed his ribs and belly. "You're my chocolate chip cookie," she whispered in his ear.

"Well, you're my little sweet potato," he murmured in return. "You know, sugar, polygamy being permitted in the hereafter, when I'm dead you can have yourself sealed to me in the temple. And you can seal Wendell to be my adopted son. I'll take you both."

"I'd rather have you now," she said.

"No, you wouldn't. I'm old and wore out; I'm crazy and crochety; I'm lewd and lascivious."

"I'd take you anyhow."

"Oh, the sin we have took up with!" he groaned. "It's the Lord's holy day, but did I pay any attention? Hell no. I climbed on this bed and fancied you and me was a stud and mare. Not so long ago you got yourself baptized. All your sins were forgiven; you were pure as driven snow. Then old Pickett came along and led you down the primrose path. I say it was a mistake getting yourself baptized, even if there wasn't any other way to get on church welfare. Now, on account of me, your forgiveness is all used up and you're worse off than you were before."

Pickett dressed and said goodby. After bobbing along the road for a quarter hour, he topped out on the cemetery hill. A sagging pigwire fence circled the cemetery, holding tumbleweeds like a net full of fish. "Ain't that something!" he exclaimed with a sweep of his arm. Silver clouds slipped over the looming rim and hurried toward the horizon. Eastward the giant land buckled: troughs and crests; rims of rock; scallops, pinnacles, buttes, peaks; plains glinting with grass; slopes frothing with juniper. He wagged his finger and asked Vincent, "See all that busted up land out there? See this here sheared-off mountain? It's vicious and murderous, isn't it? How come God would permit it on his peaceable earth, tell me that?"

"That's easy," the dog said. "Nothing to it at all. All that fracas, all them walls and erosions and busted pieces of land came on during the Lord's crucifixion. Read the Book of Mormon, Third Nephi, and see if I ain't right. And before that dreadful day, all this here was wet and wonderful, green with grass, fat with buffalo and antelope."

"You ain't telling me nothing I didn't already know," Pickett said. "Damned uppity dog. All the time gotta be instructing your betters."

Hobbling among the gravestones, noting dates, reading epitaphs, he grieved over the early deaths of little children, young wives, men cut off in full strength. Pausing by the tall marble shaft of Desmon T. Mackhalter, the most notable pioneer of the village, he put his hand over his heart and said, "Good day to you, sir. I've heard many fine things about you. Me, I come from up county a ways where there's a graveyard full of my people. You woulda knowed my grampa, Bishop Isaac Inglebar." He seated himself against the shaft and pulled a final bottle from the bag, saying, "Bishop Mackhalter was a real man. No pigshits like Delbert was called to shepherd God's flock in them days."

After he had finished the bottle he got up the courage to peer inside. He was relieved to see, instead of a four foot salamander, a hospital room in Price, he himself in bed and, standing nearby, his son Thomas in Sunday clothes and Delbert Wheatley in boots and jeans smelling of cow manure.

"First of all," said his son Thomas, who was a contractor in Pleasant Grove, "somebody is going to have to kind of steal the leg once it's amputated. It's against hospital policy to give patients back their severed members. But that's all arranged for. Now, Dad, if you'll just let them go ahead and cut it off, Bishop Wheatley has agreed to go along with your idea. He promises they'll bury it like a Christian, him and his counselors; they'll have a little private graveside service for it. And I'll pay for the casket and a stone. I promise. We all promise."

"You can't trust Delbert," Pickett said.

Thomas rolled his eyes in despair. He was beefy and short like his mother and his pate gleamed between two banks of fine brown hair.

"Listen, Pickett," Delbert said, "you know dang well if

I say we'll bury it proper, we'll do it."

"No you won't."

Delbert leaned over the hospital bed, positioning his face not five inches from Pickett's. On his nose Pickett could see porous craters and unshaved whiskers. "You old pain in the butt," he growled, "look me in the eye and call me a liar."

"I ain't got no strength," Pickett wept. "Go on, tell 'em to cut it off."

He noticed, growing between nearby graves, tiny groundhugging plants bearing orange blossoms. Struggling onto his hands and good knee, he uprooted the tiny plants and stuffed them into his breast pocket, dragging his artificial leg behind and setting the empty bottle carefully ahead each time he moved. He brought his bouquet to the grave where his leg was buried, a mound of rain-packed clay headed by a granite marker. Sitting, he tenderly arranged the mashed knot of tiny blossoms. Vincent, hunkered beside him, lifted a hind leg and idly scratched an ear.

Pickett said, "Oh, the injustices I've done Delbert, the dirty stories I've told against him, the hate I've borne in this rotten old heart. Vincent, Delbert done exactly like he promised. He had them dig a real grave, six by three. He had them bring my leg up here in the casket Thomas bought me. He had them bury it in a big box so it'll still be decent when it's time to open it up and put the rest of me in it. And, Vincent, so he told me, he dedicated the grave and promised my leg it would rise in the first resurrection.

"Oh, my God," he moaned, stretching out flat on the ground, "it'll rise and where'll the rest of me be? Nothing but manure in a privy pit; still bound in the grave."

He peered into the bottle. At first, the sun having gone behind the cliffs, he could see hardly a thing, no more than the slick yeasty amber glass. Then in a strange glow he saw a salamander of ordinary size with a stumpy tail growing where an old one had been torn off.

"I knew it!" he cried, throwing down the bottle.

"Well," Vincent said, "at least it ain't a four foot one."

"That don't matter. It gives me the sweats."

"It's a sign," Vincent said. "That rotten salamander is growing a new tail."

Pickett raised the bottle to his eye and this time he saw three posts rising from sight through the upper side of the bottle. Men's feet were nailed to the posts.

"I ain't man enough," he groaned. "I ain't got the courage."

"Give it another try," Vincent suggested.

He looked again and he saw Jesus with a bloody forehead. He put down the bottle and wept, "Lord, don't forget old Pickett."